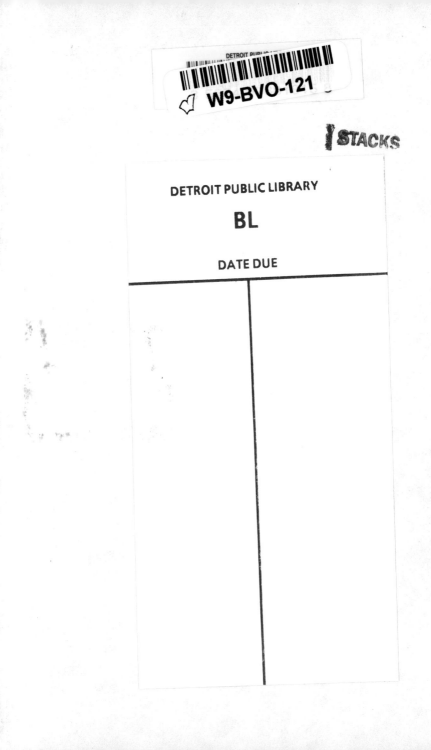

THE STAR OF LIFE

THE STAR OF LIFE

By Edmond Hamilton

Kirk Hammond was a man alone.

He had been chosen to ride in the first manned satellite to go out around the Moon and back to Earth. But when the satellite failed to orbit properly, it went on past the Moon into the vastness of outer space, and a whole world watched helplessly as he was borne toward an unthinkably lonely death.

Yet destiny decreed that Kirk Hammond should suffer, not death but a pseudo-death. And he awoke from it to find that a hundred centuries had passed and that the space age which had begun in the 20th Century had now grown into a vast galactic civilization that had carried the sons of Earth to countless stars and worlds. But, unexpectedly, the conquest of space had changed Man himself, and the human race had become not one but several species.

Hammond was plunged into the climactic struggle between the new races. And in his quest with a desperate band for the mysterious Star of Life that was the key to the struggle, in his relations with the strange and beautiful Thayn Marden who was not a human woman, in his odyssey through the mighty suns and earthly worlds of the galaxy, a man of the 20th Century found himself facing the dangers of the great space age which he himself helped pioneer.

THE STAR

OF

LIFE

by   *copy-1*

EDMOND HAMILTON

A Torquil Book

DISTRIBUTED BY
DODD, MEAD & COMPANY
New York

To Leigh

Chapter 1

HE WAS more alone than anyone had ever been before. He was alone, and he was dead.

His heart beat. His eyes saw, and his ears heard, and he felt. And yet, thought Kirk Hammond, he was a dead man and already in his tomb, this spheroid of magnesium and steel, this bubble of air and light flying silently out into the deeps of space, the vast and illimitable oceans of night.

It was funny. It was so funny that the sun and moon and stars were screaming with soundless laughter. A great nation had aspired, and many hundreds of brilliant men had worried and sweated, and many millions of dollars had been spent, and all of it just to give Kirk Hammond a funeral liked nobody had ever had before.

He laughed about it.

He sobbed.

The radio was buzzing, the last thin thread of coded sounds that still bound him to Earth. Soon, very soon, that umbilical cord of sound that tied him to his birth-world would break, and he would be dead to Earth.

"*Canaveral to Explorer Nineteen, 17:44. The President announces award of the Congressional Medal of Honor to Kirk Hammond. The President adds, 'With it goes a nation's thanks to its hero.' End message.*"

That's fine, thought Hammond. I'm a hero. I've got a medal. They might as well have called it a posthumous award. That's what it is.

The radio buzzed again, almost at once.

"*Canaveral to Explorer Nineteen, 17:47. World-wide gatherings are praying for you, Hammond. Every church, every creed, is holding special prayer services. End of message."*

Prayers for the dead, he thought dully. That was nice of them. Very nice.

He could imagine the great wave of emotion sweeping around the world, the horror and pity at his fate. Those people didn't know him. Until the firing of Explorer Nineteen they had never heard of him. But now that he was trapped by a doom unlike any that had ever befallen a man before, their emotions would be real enough.

Hammond was tired. For more than a hundred hours he had been sitting strapped into his chair in this little sphere, and his body was cramped and numb. His mind was numb, too. He had had too much, in too short a time. The shock of the first firing. The blackout. The coming to, the struggle to breathe, to think, to raise his hand to the radio key and send back the signal that he still lived. The fear, and the gasping, and the tearing at his entrails, and then the thunder of God when the second stage of the rocket let go and hurled him into complete unconsciousness. He had come out of that shaken and sick, but with nothing inside him broken. And then had come the tensest wait of all, the waiting for the third stage to fire, the one that would hurl the little spherical shell of Hammond's satellite into its pre-calculated orbit. An orbit that would carry Kirk Hammond, first of all men, out around the Moon and back again to Earth.

Since years before, since 1957 and the first Russian Sputnik, they had been sending up satellites. First, in orbit around the Earth, unmanned ones to begin with and then when the ejection-escape mechanism had been perfected, with a man inside. Then the first unmanned satellite had been sent out in an orbit around the Moon. Now a man was going out, not to land upon the Moon but to fly out around it and back again and to land—if the ejection gimmick worked!— safe and alive on Earth. And Hammond was the man, the man who had waited tautly for that third stage to fire as he whirled up high over Earth in the steep trajectory.

Too soon! He had known from the very instant that the third stage exploded that something had gone wrong with the timer-relays, that the third stage had fired too soon. It had happened before, when satellites were launched. The curve was too steep, and the orbit was all wrong. Explorer Nineteen would not come nearly as close to the Moon as planned. It would be far enough to keep clear of the Moon's gravitational pull. And that meant. . . .

It meant that the satellite would not swing around the Moon at all but would pass it, and would go on, and on, and on.

The radio buzzed again.

"Canaveral to Explorer Nineteen, 18:02. Your hourly report is two minutes overdue. Please give your readings. End message."

Hammond smiled mirthlessly. That was John Willing. He could imagine Willing down there in Communications, sweating blood, keeping up a pretense with him, trying to pretend to him that everything was still routine, trying to keep his mind off the other thing. He switched on and tapped out the figures that he read off the meters, the dust-density, radiation, temperature sunside and darkside. Before he continued, he turned for a look back. The aluminum frame of the ejection seat, the seat in which he had been doubled for all these hours, swivelled easily in gimbals and he looked back through the Number Four filter-glass port.

A gigantic shadowed skullface glared at him, filling much of the star-decked black firmament. It was a little off to his right and he could not see that it was any smaller than an hour before, but he knew it was. The Moon would get smaller and smaller as Explorer Nineteen went on away from it, but after a certain point he would not be alive to see its diminishing. He looked beyond it to Earth. It was nothing but a biggish fuzzy greenish globe. He tried again to think how great a thing it was to be first of men to go out this far from it.

He tried, and he couldn't, it wouldn't work, and oh God

why had he ever left? A man had to die sometime but no-body had ever died this way, alone in the dark lifeless emptiness a million miles from all his kind. A warm and passionate awareness of Earth, of all its ways that he had al-ways taken for granted, arose in Hammond. Soft rain in spring nights, old trees beside a sleeping farm, the crude, brassy, surging human noises of a big city street, the wash and roll of the sea, the ways of winds and waves and birds. You had so much when you were living, that you never thought about until you were dead. Could the dead think? One of them could. Kirk Hammond could.

He clenched his fist and made his fingers stop their trem-bling before he sent the last sentences of his report, giving his visual reactions. The answer came quickly.

"Canaveral to Explorer Nineteen, 18:24. Report received. Do not lose hope, Hammond. Staff astronomers state that there is a chance unknown gravitational factors might bring you back into orbit. End message."

Hammond smiled a crooked smile again. He touched the key rapidly.

"Explorer Nineteen to Canaveral, 18:33. Don't feel you have to cheer me up, Willing. I learned my astrogation at Base too well. I've calculated the orbit of this satellite and it's going a long way before it comes back again. End mes-sage."

A long way, yes. The calculations, the frantic figures on the sheets that had slowly spelled out his doom to him, were still on his lap. With the cold finality of mathematics, they told what would happen to him. Explorer Nineteen was go-ing far out beyond the Moon, very far. Its orbit would be a vastly elongated ellipse and that meant that somewhere out there it would turn and fall back and take up a far-swinging orbit around the Sun like that of a periodic comet. Once in a century or so it might come comparatively near to Earth.

Once in a century . . . Hammond's air-supply, not to men-tion water and food, had been calculated for a six-day swing out around the Moon and back again. And the six days were almost gone. He looked down at the actuating lever of the ejection-seat, the gadget that had been meant to bring him safely down by parachute when Explorer Nineteen returned to Earth. It would never be used, now. He was not going to return to Earth.

"Canaveral to Explorer Nineteen, 18:55. Your call is weaker but we can still work you. Are your batteries fading? Any message? End message."

Yes, Hammond thought, he had a message for them. He wanted to send it, to shout it, to scream it. He wanted to tell them to get him out of this neat, glittering little tomb, to get him back to Earth, somehow, anyhow. But there was no somehow. No help could reach him. There just wasn't any way. Someday, in the future, there might be manned rocket-ships that could do it, but not now. All the peoples of Earth could do, now, was to watch and listen helplessly as Explorer Nineteen bore him inexorably away into the darkness and the death.

Hammond felt panic rising in him fast. He must not let it master him. It would not help one little bit for him to sob his guts out over the radio. He had asked for this job, and he had known it was dangerous, and he might as well end up like a man and not a crybaby.

But he distrusted himself. Sooner or later hysteria might get the best of him, and start him to screaming across the void.

With sudden decision, Hammond tapped the key.

"Explorer Nineteen to Canaveral. Yes, my batteries are about gone. This will be my last contact. Don't let this accident stop you in the future. Good luck to all the guys who follow me. End message."

And as he finished, Hammond convulsively wrenched off the shielding and smashed at the tubes with a blind, quivering blow of his fist. Then he sat shaking. The batteries were not dead, but the radio was. No more talking back and forth. No danger now of breaking down and bawling and making a spectacle of himself. Back there on Earth, they'd think it an heroic last message. They wouldn't know that dread of panic had dictated it.

He was alone now. Really alone.

He looked through the port in front of him, at the glittering chains of stars. He was going to die out here where no man had ever died before. Well, there was a certain distinction in that.

Hammond felt very tired. It was odd, that with death looming you could still feel fatigue. But he did. He had sat in the cramped seat here inside the satellite for more than a hundred hours, and his body ached, and his brain felt numb. He had come a long way from the boy in an Ohio town who had yelled in excitement at the news of the first Sputnik. Had it been worth it, the struggle through Tech, the grinding nights of study, the planning and the toil, just for this?

He tried to imagine what they'd be saying about him back on Earth now. Thank God he had no one back there to grieve too deeply. The death of his parents in that auto-crash a few years ago was one reason, he knew, why Willing had picked him out of the final group of volunteers. But what was Willing saying, what were the crowds saying, the radio and TV announcers? It didn't matter. When he broke the radio, when he severed his last link with Earth, Earth and its people had somehow ceased to matter any more.

He was Kirk Hammond, alone in the universe and soon to die.

How soon?

Hammond studied the gauges of the oxygenator. He had less than two hours' oxygent left, even counting the small supply in the ejection-gimmick's tank. He wished he had even less time. He was afraid, terribly afraid, of going mad before he died.

"But why wait?"

It was as though a voice had spoken inside his tired brain. Why wait for the inevitable torture of asphyxiation? All he had to do was to open the hatch and the airless cold of space would end it all for him with merciful painlessness.

Hammond laid his hand on the heavy dogs of the hatch. Surely this was forgivable, this escape from madness and strangulation?

All of a sudden, in his brain the blind will to live frantically suggested impossible hopes.

"Don't do it! Don't open the hatch! Maybe the satellite will still turn back—maybe someone will come in a rocket—maybe—"

Crazy, impossible, he knew those hopes to be. It was only his subconscious putting up a last fight against his reason. Hammond fought down the clamorous voices. He had to do this thing quickly, or he would not do it at all. He began undogging the hatch with nervous haste.

The hatch went *pung!* and opened a tiny crack. Air started to whistle out of it in a needle-like jet. Hammond opened it no further, for to do so would mean an explosive decompression. He sat back, his shoulders sagging. He had come a long way and he was very tired.

He suddenly felt an awful and agonizing sensation of cold invade his whole body. This death was not as painless as he had expected!

That was his last thought.

Chapter 2

THERE HAD been only darkness, but now there was pain also.

He wished that the pain would go away, and cease to trouble his comfortable not-being, not-feeling. But it did not go away. Instead, it got worse, a fiery, rasping agony of his lungs each time he tried to breathe.

How could he breathe when he had died? That was Hammond's first dazed and bewildered thought. The thing was impossible. Yet his lungs were pumping in and out, burning up, gasping for air that was not there.

Hammond's brain struggled numbly with the problem. He tried to open his eyes, and could not. He could not move a muscle. But he could feel. Each moment the fiery agony in his lungs spread and crept in his body, and now he could also feel that the metal arms of the ejection-seat on which his hands rested were blistering hot.

He could hear, also. There was a thin, hissing screaming sound somewhere close to his ears. It went on and on without varying in pitch or volume.

The pain very swiftly became a torment too great to be borne. He was strangling, suffocating, he was going to die again. It was not fair that he should have to die again. He made a convulsive effort, and his body moved jerkily.

His eyes opened.

He saw through a red haze. He was still seated in the ejection-seat of the satellite. Its hatch was open a tiny crack and the screaming sound came from that. Thin air, air so thin and ozone-laden that his lungs could not breathe it, was streaming in through it. The air or mockery of air was utterly cold, yet the metal of the satellite itself was scorching hot.

Hammond was only one-third consciousness but he knew that he was dying for lack of oxygen. The drill back at Rocket Base had been stamped deep into his memory, and a phrase from it flashed across his fading mind. The Time of Useful Consciousness. The time a man had to save himself when his oxygen ran out. Even at five miles up in the atmosphere, it was less than two minutes. Further up, in space equivalent, it could be counted in seconds. His seconds were running out. Remember the drill. . . .

He remembered. He groped with leaden arms and hands that felt like muffs, for the oxygen tube of the ejection capsule. He got it into his mouth, and then fumbled blindly at the valve. His fingers would not work right, he had to paw the little metal handle as a dog might until it opened.

16

The blessed relief of oxygen pouring into his starved, super-heated lungs set him to quivering and shaking.

He sat breathing, trembling, looking with vacant and uncomprehending eyes at the blazing star-fields that slid by outside the forward port as the satellite slowly rotated. Then, swinging slow and majestically into view, came a gray-green thing so vast that it completely filled the port. A cloudy, striated surface swept past the glass, and then a curved limb and then the stars again.

Hammond watched, numbly. In less than a minute the phenomenon was repeated.

Now the first faint curiosity stirred in his dulled brain. The oxygen was taking effect, and he could think and wonder, and it was about the vast gray-green object that he wondered. He hitched the chair forward in its gimbals so that he could get a wider view through the port.

A hoarse cry burst from Hammond. Gigantic in starry space beneath the satellite, arcing vastly across the heavens, was a familiar spherical bulk of gray and green.

"Earth." He whispered the word, but it was only an automatic recognition, he did not believe it yet.

The glass was blistering his face, the whole satellite was heating up by the minute, yet he would not take his face away from the glass until the revolving of the satellite brought the vast bulk again into view. And after this second look, there was no doubt about it at all. His brain suddenly clamored, shocked into full wakefulness. He yelled the name this time. He waited, trembling, unbelieving, until the rotation of the satellite brought Earth, or him, around again. This time he studied its surface with more care. He estimated that Explorer Nineteen was no more than forty miles above the surface of Earth, and revolving around it at a velocity in excess of twenty thousand miles an hour. He had been headed for the outer reaches of the Solar System, when he had opened the hatch. He had been certain that Nineteen would go out and out, for days, for years. There seemed no way in which it could return to Earth. Yet, somehow, it had.

"—a chance unknown gravitational factors might bring you back into orbit—"

He remembered that penultimate message from Canaveral. He had thought that they were merely trying to soften the end for him with a little hope. But maybe they had been right? One thing was sure. Nineteen *had* fallen back toward Earth, and was now spinning around it in a tightening spiral.

But there was a bigger mystery. He had sought quick death by opening the hatch in space. He had died. Yet now he was alive.

How could a man be frozen instantly in death, and then live again?

Solemn, majestic, the vast sphere of Earth returned into his view each few minutes, and he clung, and gasped the life-giving oxygen, and stared. His body was one great ache, and the scorching breath from hot metal and the icy blast of thin air that screamed through the partly-opened hatch simultaneously blistered and froze him.

Hammond's dazed mind groped for some explanation of the incredible fact of his awakening. Suppose, instead of being really dead, he had only been in a state of ultra-hypothermia? Hypothermia, or radically lowered body temperatures, was a common tool of medicine and surgery these days. The first experiments back in the '40's and early '50's had proved that you could almost literally freeze a man and then bring him back to life by applying warmth, if you did it right. Even back at the time of the first Sputnik, American scientists had frozen dogs and then re-started their heart action after an hour or so. The Russians were supposed to have done the same thing with people, and their claims for their hypothermic techniques had been astonishing.

Hypothermia . . . And what, Hammond thought, if the thing were done suddenly as it had never been done before, as it could not be done in any laboratory, by the absolute cold of space? A super-hypothermia acting with incredible speed, freezing every cell in his body rigid before any cellular or organic damage could begin, plunging him into a rock-like state of suspended animation. And then, when the satellite dropped back toward Earth, wouldn't the thin air of the upper atmosphere and the increasing warmth of the friction-heated sphere gradually revive him?

It all went whirling through Hammond's brain, the instinctive attempt of a 20th Century man to find a rational explanation for the incredible. And then he forgot it. For he suddenly realized that however he had come back to life he had done so only to die again very quickly, unless he did something. The satellite was getting hotter by the minute. He could no longer stand the touch of the hot metal. As it whirled round and round Earth in the upper atmosphere, friction was heating Explorer Nineteen to the point where it would soon burn up like a falling meteor.

He would burn with it, if he didn't get out.

Until now, he had been too amazed and numb with wonder to feel a personal concern. But now the instinct of self-preservation set up a frantic clamor in his mind. By some strange freak of cosmic factors, Explorer Nineteen had been brought back to Earth. It was up to him now to get out of it in time. His body still felt leaden, his head heavy to bursting, but he began an urgent study of his exact situation.

Below lay the sunlit side of Earth, most of it veiled in drifting cloud. He thought he could recognize the coastline of the Iberian Peninsula through a gap in the clouds. If that were so, he was moving westward over the Atlantic toward North America, that was now on the night side. He must time his ejection from the satellite to make sure he came down over land.

As Hammond's fingers fumbled clumsily over the levers and switches, an oddly humorous thought shot across his mind.

"Won't they be surprised when their dead hero chutes down alive? Wonder if they'll take that medal away from me?"

The chair in which Hammond sat strapped was suspended

so that it hung inside a semi-globular plastic bowl, inside the satellite. Now, as the controls responded, other curved plastic sections swung up from underneath him, enclosing him and the chair and the ejection emergency gimmicks, inside a round plastic sphere. That type of enclosure had been mandatory in planning for a man to bail out of a satellite.

Hammond kept the oxygen-tube in his mouth, and peered through both the plastic and the filter-glass port together, to estimate Nineteen's progress around the Earth.

"Damn those clouds! I won't be able to see any lights of cities when I do pass over!"

Nineteen was rushing on toward the dark shadow of Earth, toward its nighted side. And below, the clouds were an almost solid mass.

Inside the closer confines of the plastic sphere, it was getting hotter very rapidly. His skin felt parched and withering. And now, with sudden sharp alarm, he saw that the aluminum rim of the filter port was glowing faintly in the darkness. Explorer Nineteen, sinking into denser atmosphere with each pass around the Earth, was beginning to reach the critical stage of frictional heat.

Hammond resisted a strong temptation to pull the ejection lever at once. He must be over mid-Atlantic, it was night, he might not be picked up for a long time. No, wait—wait till he was sure he was over land.

But could he wait? The sinister, faint red glow was suffusing the whole skin of the satellite now, and his brain reeled from the heat. He hung on and waited. It was all guess work for he hadn't been able to gauge speed and altitude too closely, but he thought he must be already sweeping across the coast. Wait a little, and be sure. . . .

Hammond yanked one of the two levers set in the central axle of the plastic sphere's gimbal framework.

Nothing happened.

Panic clamored again in him. If he couldn't get the ejection bay open, he'd never get out. Frantically, he tugged the lever.

This time, it took hold. With a grating sound audible even over the thin screaming of air, the whole bottom plate of the satellite vanished, unlinked and then blown clear by a small explosive charge. He could now look right down through the plastic, right down past his feet, at the cloudy darkness below. His fingers gripped the other lever, the one with the big "E" on it. It was too hot to hold, everything was getting too hot, he couldn't wait any longer, surely he must be well over land by now.

Hammond pulled the "E" lever.

He was flung violently against the straps as the charge shot the ejection-capsule out of the now-open satellite. The plastic bubble whirled over and over, falling. His leaden hulk of a body rocked back and forth and the oxygen tube fell out of his mouth. He groped for it but there was a fiery mist obscuring his vision and he could not find it. His breathing became agonized again. The pain in his lungs made him flail his hands frantically till they touched the dangling tube. He got it back into his mouth and then almost lost it as another sharp shock threw him against the chair-straps again.

He did not quite lose the tube. And presently his mind cleared a little. The ejection-bubble was not now spinning. He looked up and saw the blaze of the starry night sky steady over his head, for the first time since his awakening. Against the star-fields up there a great round darkness bulked, and Hammond knew what it was. The parachute of the ejection-bubble had opened right on time, and he was drifting steadily down toward the nighted surface of the Earth.

He felt a shivering relief. Until now, almost everything he had done had been semi-mechanical, from habit of training. But now the thin edge of excitement rose in his numb brain.

"I'm going to make it—"

Blood pounded through his veins. He felt horribly weak but an access of new life swept away the leaden heaviness. Hammond looked eagerly down. There was nothing but the dark clouds. Until he got down through them, there would be nothing.

It seemed to take the parachuted plastic sphere a long time to float down into the clouds. His heart suddenly began to hammer violently, and he took the oxygen tube out of his mouth. No need for that now. . . .

He kept peering down, alert for the first lights that he would see when he came out of the clouds.

He saw no lights.

There was only the solid, frustrating darkness, and he could not even be sure that he was out of the clouds yet. Yet he must be, he ought to be clear and able to see by now. Then, suddenly, his eyes caught a vague loom below, a faintly glistening expanse that made contrast with the darkness. Of a sudden, badly startled, he realized that the glistening was nòt far beneath but was close under him, and he realized what it was.

It was the sea. He had misjudged and jumped the satellite too soon.

The plastic ball hit the water and was swept away on a long wave-crest. Hammond just in time remembered the parachute-release and actuated it, cutting loose the vast billowing fabric before it smothered down on him. The ejection-sphere had been designed for a possible water landing. Its air-intakes were opposite its slightly weighted "keel". It bobbed up and down on the dark ocean with Hammond in it feeling like a minnikin in a floating bottle.

Hammond sagged in the straps, feeling now a horrible reaction. He slept.

When he awoke, he thought that hours had passed. A wind was tossing the sea, and the motion of the sphere was sickening. But the wind had swept away the clouds overhead. The stars shone now across the whole sky. He peered westward. Surely he could not be far from the coast. He saw a dark, low line of blackness where stars and ocean met. He felt sure it was the coast, and the wind was driving the bubble in that direction.

Hammond looked up at the sky. Incredible, to think he had come back from out there, surviving the pseudo-death of space, wakening again when some strange quirk of circumstance had brought the satellite back toward Earth. What could have brought it back?

But that tremendous question faded from Hammond's mind as he continued to stare at the sky. His gaze became fixed upon the stars in the northern heavens.

There was something wrong about the stars. Something impossibly, insanely wrong.

Chapter 3

HAMMOND KNEW the constellations thoroughly. A close knowledge of star-groups was a part of the astrogation course that had been pounded into him and the other volunteers before they ever went to Canaveral. And the northern constellations, glittering low above the sea, were not right. Ursa Major and Draco and the others were all revolving slowly around the celestial northern pole. But the center of that movement, the pole-star, was no longer Polaris. It was a fainter star that he recognized as Delta Cygni, many degrees across the heavens from the former polar star.

He could not quite believe it at first. But as the plastic sphere bobbled and drifted on toward the land, as he watched the stars up there moving like cosmic clock-hands, there could no longer be any doubt. Hammond faced a staggering realization.

"But that would mean that hundreds of years have gone by. No, not hundreds—thousands!"

The celestial pole constantly changed position in the heavens, due to the precession of the equinoxes. Every twenty-seven thousand years, the pole described a small circle in the sky. If the pole was now at or near Delta Cygni, it had described more than a third of that circle. And that would mean that something like ten thousand years had passed since he had last checked the northern stars.

Ten thousand years? It was too ridiculous, too fantastic. There was some aberration of the starlight, or something wrong with his eyes. There was no possible way in which such a vast period of time could have elapsed since he had taken off, since. . . .

Hammond's angry mental repudiation of what he saw suddenly received a check. An icy feeling invaded his mind. Maybe there was an explanation that he hadn't thought of, a stupefying one. That frozen sleep, the ultra-hypothermia that had gripped him in suspended animation in the satellite—he had assumed without thinking about it that it had been comparatively brief in duration. A few days, perhaps even a week, but no more. But had he any reason for assuming that? The absolute cold of space, gripping every cell in his body when he opened the hatch out there, was a changeless thing. It could have held him frozen a year as easily as a day. A year—or a thousand years.

How long had he lain in frozen sleep?

The glittering hands of the vast star-clock answered him, but he could not accept that terrifying answer.

And yet—it would explain the thing that was otherwise incomprehensible, the return of Explorer Nineteen to Earth. When he had opened the hatch to avoid a torturing end, the satellite had been beyond the Moon, on its way out into space in a vast elliptical orbit. He had calculated that it would return on that orbit in many years, and that after returning many times in many centuries it might fall into the gravitational field of Earth. If that had happened, if the star-clock told true time, for a hundred centuries Kirk Hammond had sat frozen in the sphere until at last it swung so close to its parent planet that it was pulled down into the atmosphere, where frictional heat had revived him.

Hammond's mind recoiled from the thought. He could not, would not, believe it. If that were true, countless generations had risen and died on Earth since he had ridden the roaring flames up from Canaveral. If it were true, whole races and empires could have flashed forth and blown away like candles on the wind during that frozen coma that had seemed so brief to him. And if it were true, all on Earth whom Kirk Hammond had known were dead for ages, their dust dispersed and their memory forgotten.

"John Willing, and Barnett, and Cray, and that girl in Cleveland, and—"

No. There was some other explanation, there had to be. He would find out when he reached land. He would laugh then at having had such a fantastic thought. Willing would laugh, they would all laugh.

He peered toward the land with an increased tenseness and urgency. He wanted to reach it as soon as possible, to disprove the nightmare thought he had been afflicted with.

The dark line of the coast was thicker, higher against the starlit sea. Presently he made out a spectral white line below it and knew it to be surf. A sharp alarm jabbed him as he thought of the bobbing plastic sphere being hurled against rocks. His alarm increased when he came nearer and could make out the irregular blacker blots of jagged rock around which the surf was creaming. He unloosened his straps and made ready to scramble out and swim, as the long swell bore the sphere forward in a smooth rush.

There was no shock of impact. The surf sucked the sphere in between two craggy boulders and deposited it on a little beach of sand as gently as a mother would put down a child. Hammond had the sphere open instantly. He jumped out and fell onto his face, filling his mouth with wet sand. His legs could no more support him than a pair of wet strings. He had forgotten how many hours he had sat cramped in the satellite—not to mention how long he had remained rigid in frozen sleep out there in the gloom and glare of space.

He lay in the sand unable to move. He gave up.

Then the cold flood of the surf washed over him and he was nerved to effort again by the shock of the chill water and the fear of being swept back into the ocean. He still could not stand, but he crawled and floundered further up the beach until he reached a towering rock with rough eroded sides that he could cling to. After a few minutes Hammond got hold of the rock and hauled himself up to a standing position. His legs were steady enough to hold him if he leaned against the rough stone. Thus leaning, he turned his head to peer again at those incredible northern constellations.

But as he turned his head, he glimpsed the firefly lights.

They looked like that—three or four fireflies flitting about far out over the starlit sea whence he had come. They seemed to dance and waver, to spin and mill and spread out in a pattern of increasing area. He knew that they could not really be glowing insects, so they must be lighted planes of some kind, but they did not look or fly like any planes he knew.

Without warning, a powerful hand grabbed Hammond's right wrist from behind.

"What the devil—!" he exclaimed, starting to whirl around.

He did not complete the movement. His right arm was instantly drawn up into a painful hammerlock behind his back. Unable to break free, Hammond wildly squirmed his head around to look up at his assailant.

The man who held him was a big hulking individual in loose dark jacket and trousers. He topped Hammond by at least a foot. He had short-cropped, bristling black hair partly covered by a tight turban over the back of his skull. But what made Hammond gasp in astonishment was his face. It was a massive, battered-looking face that reminded him of an oldtime boxer's, not at all unlikable even though his narrowed eyes were glaring down at Hammond with hostility and suspicion. What was odd about it was the color it showed in the starlight.

The man's face was pale blue.

Holding Hammond like a child, the blue man pointed with his free hand in the direction of the distant firefly lights and spoke harshly. Hammond could not understand a word he said. It was not English or any other language he had ever heard. And standing there on what should have been the familiar American coast, facing this man of a race and language he had never known, there fell upon Hammond a terrible conviction that the hands of the star-clock had told true time and that his frozen sleep had indeed carried him across an age.

The blue man seemed upset by Hammond's obvious lack of understanding, and puzzled by something else. He pointed to Hammond's head and then to his own, then once more at the few fireflies flickering out there over the sea.

"*Vramen! Vramen!*" he repeated sharply, in a tone that might be either a suspicious challenge or a warning.

Hammond could not understand at all. Again the man pointed to his own head and then he pointed at Hammond's, questioningly. That made Hammond look at him more closely. He saw now that the tight turban that partially covered the blue man's skull was of a gleaming metallic fabric.

"*Vramen!*" yelled the other suddenly, pointing eastward.

Hammond looked and saw that the distant fireflies were now separating. One still hovered low above the sea out there. But the others were now quartering westward over the ocean, in a search-pattern that was rapidly approaching the coast.

The blue man's face expressed indecision, a mingled doubt and apprehension. Abruptly he dragged Hammond down to the ground into the deep black shadow beside the big boulder. Hammond struggled angrily but the blue man held him without effort and fiercely motioned him to be still.

Hammond looked up and saw one of the fireflies approaching at a low altitude. It was a craft that flew quite silently and at great speed. He could make out a long, transparent hull or fuselage—the light from inside it, and its darting, searching movements, were what had made him think of fireflies. Beside him, the blue man had suddenly released his hold and was frantically active. He had unwound part of his metallic cloth turban and was using a thin knife to cut off the length he had unwound. It was so incomprehensible a thing to do that Hammond forgot to take advantage of his momentary freedom and gawked in wonder.

And suddenly Hammond heard a clear voice speak inside his mind. It was a commanding voice resounding in his brain, carrying an hypnotic weight of authority.

"Come from hiding and show yourself," it commanded. "Signal your whereabouts to us!"

Hammond, totally without volition, found himself getting up and starting mechanically out of the shadow toward the starlit beach. The blue man grabbed his ankles and tripped him. As Hammond sprawled, the man hastily wrapped around his head the length of metallic cloth he had cut from his own turban. At once the hypnotic mental command stopped.

Hammond found himself shaking violently, as though drawn back from the edge of an abyss. The whole swift experience had been unearthly in nature. He lay in the shadow, trembling like a hunted animal. What kind of an Earth had he been thrown into?

His companion seemed to take it all as a matter of course. The blue man crouched, looking up shrewdly at the firefly craft that kept darting to and fro. Those flitting, silent fliers were moving along the coast in a continuing regular search-pattern. Now Hammond began to understand a little. That eery mental command must have come from the searching craft—and because it was mental there had been no language difficulty, a thought directly transmitted would not require any translation. The metallic turban was of a material that provided shielding against that hypnotic attack. The blue man wore it for that reason, and a length of it had screened Hammond from it.

The blue man now uttered a grunt of satisfaction. The firefly craft were flying straight back to the one that still hovered far out over the sea. They had, obviously, given up the search for the time being.

Sitting up, the blue man looked at Hammond. He still looked wary. But he seemed tremendously curious and interested, rather than hostile. Finally he touched his own chest and spoke.

"Rab Quobba," he said.

That, at least, was unmistakable. Hammond touched his own chest and spoke his name.

"Hammond?" the other repeated, accenting it oddly. He stared puzzledly at Hammond, and then he pointed west toward the dark land and asked, "Do Rurooma?"

That meant nothing at all. Hammond made a shrugging gesture to show his ignorance.

Rab Quobba frowned. He was a big and formidable man but he did not look to Hammond like an intellectual type, and he was clearly out of his depth. He pointed inland again and repeated, "Rurooma? Dal Vramen?"

It sounded to Hammond as though he was being asked if he came from the place whence the searching firefly craft had come. He could not be sure, but he took a chance. He shook his head.

Quobba frowned and hitched his feet and then seemed to make up his mind. He motioned to Hammond to accompany him, and started southward with long strides along the beach. Hammond hesitated a moment and then went with him. He had not the faintest idea where they were going or who this big man with the oddly bluish skin might be. He had been pitchforked into an Earth that was as incomprehensible to him as another planet. But he had sensed menace in the searching firefly craft—that uncanny hypnotic attack had been upsetting. And Rab Quobba had been friendly, at least so far.

He took a dozen steps and then stopped, swaying. His legs were too weak and leaden, he couldn't keep up. Quobba turned swiftly and came back to him. The blue man seemed to take in Hammond's weakness. He grunted and put one arm around Hammond to help him along.

Quobba kept wherever possible in the shadow of the great boulders that studded the beach. He moved fast between patches of shadow, and he kept a wary eye on the fireflies out there over the sea. He seemed in a sweating hurry to get where they were going. A hazy dimness settled over Hammond's brain. His strength was running out and he moved his legs like an ill-made mechanical doll, his weight hanging more and more on Quobba's massive arm. Then for a moment he was startled out of his daze. Far to the west inland, a sword of light struck upward into the starry sky. It was like a monster lightning-bolt going up, leaving a livid fiery trail. As it faded out there came a distant twanging sound.

Quobba, in answer to Hammond's wondering look, pointed briefly westward and then straight upward at the stars. Hammond wondered. That fiery flash had looked like the trail of an ascending space-ship. Then, if all those centuries had really passed, men had fully conquered space by now? Perhaps even interstellar space?

But if that were so, why were some of the men of Earth furtively hiding—and from whom?

He was reeling and knew he could go no farther when Quobba finally stopped. They were in the shadow of a huge boulder, on a rocky ridge well inland from the coast. The blue man looked carefully all around the starry sky. Then he spoke sharply.

"Shau Tammas! Quobba—aben!"

A section in the side of the great boulder swung inward, disclosing a dark aperture. At first, Hammond thought that his eyes were playing tricks on him. Then he realized that the whole boulder must be a hollow camouflage. He had little time to look, for Quobba drew him hastily inside. There was a sighing sound as the aperture closed behind them, and they were in utter darkness. Then a globe overhead flashed into light.

Hammond stood rocking on his feet and staring. The interior of the big fake boulder was a small room. There were three other men in it, men dressed also in dark jackets and slacks. Two of them were quite ordinary young men of his own age. The other man, whom Quobba was addressing as Tammas, was not ordinary at all. He was a wizened little chap with a wrinkled golden-yellow face and beady black eyes, yet with no Oriental cast of countenance whatever. He exclaimed in wonder at the sight of Hammond, and the other two stared in dumb amazement.

Hammond's dazed eyes swept from the men to the big instrument that occupied much of the room. It looked like a six-inch refracting telescope mounted on a heavy pedestal, and yet there were things about it that didn't fit a telescope at all. He noticed that a section of the ceiling above it was so mounted that it could be swung aside, allowing the big tube to sweep the sky. The unfamiliar instrument, the unfamiliar technology it represented, completed Hammond's bewilderment.

Quobba took the turban off Hammond's head and drew him by the arm toward a well-mouth that yawned at one side of the chamber. A narrow spiral stair of metal dropped down this vertical shaft. Hammond went down it with the blue man going ahead and reaching back to steady him. The wizened little yellow man named Shau Tammas came after them with monkey-like agility. There was bright white light below, and they went down into the light, into a great room or hall that had been cut or blasted somehow out of solid rock.

The room was big and lofty. Brilliant white globes in the rock ceiling shed an almost shadowless illumination. Around the walls were unfamiliar machines, tables of whirring instruments, glittering metal assemblies. There were more than a score of people working busily at the machines—most of them were men, but some were women who wore shirts and shorts. The majority of these people were of a perfectly familiar type but there were a few who looked as unusual

31

as Quobba and Tammas—a couple of stocky men with dull red skins, a lanky hollow-eyed man with a curious smooth gray complexion. They turned from their work to look at Hammond in surprise and quick-rising alarm.

He stared back, seeing their faces as though in a dream. He knew that he was nearly out. He would have sunk to the floor if Rab Quobba had not steadied him as he led him across the hall. Behind him wondering and excited men and women followed, their voices rising in a buzzing chatter. They went through connecting rock-cut halls to a smaller chamber that seemed their destination. Here were shelves of curious metal-bound books, wall-charts of astronomical diagrams, a couple of littered desks.

"Ez Jon Wilson, lanf do nos Hoomen," Quobba said to Hammond, pointing to the man who was coming toward them.

Jon Wilson was past middle age. He overwhelmingly reminded Hammond of someone, and suddenly he remembered. There had been a man named John Brown of Harper's Ferry, a long time ago. A harsh, fanatic leader. He had seen pictures of that man and this one was like him—the same gaunt narrow face of iron-hard planes, the same iron-gray hair, the deep hollow-caverned eyes, everything but the beard. The impact of those eyes was like a blow, and in them was an alert anxiety as he looked at Hammond.

There was a girl at his side, slender in her brief garment, her dark hair falling to touch her shoulders. She was pretty as a hawk, and her dark eyes were wide with wonder.

"Ez an do Vramen?" she asked quickly of Rab Quobba.

"Nun, Iva!" the blue man said. His battered face was earnest as he made rapid explanations, pointing excitedly upward toward the rock ceiling.

To Hammond it was more like a dream every minute. The whole scene was blurring. He had kept going on sheer nerve, but now the inevitable reaction hit him like a mountain falling on him. He tried to hold on, to fight back the shapeless darkness. He became aware that an altercation was going on. A tall hard-eyed man with sandy hair was speaking rapidly to Jon Wilson, gesturing at Hammond with suspicion in every line of his face. Suspicion, and hate.

"Dito, ez fa Vramen!" the sandy-haired man said, and a mutter of agreement came from those crowded in behind Hammond. But Quobba shook his head in angry denial.

"Ez nun, Lund!"

But the sandy-haired man only talked louder, against Quobba.

It was pretty obvious, Hammond thought, that at least some of these people thought he was a spy or ally of some enemy of theirs called the Vramen. And, ignorant as he was of their language, how was he going to tell them the truth about himself?

Even more important, how was he going to make them believe it?

Chapter 4

HAMMOND'S EYES fell upon the astronomical charts on the wall, and a thought came into his mind. He went unsteadily toward the charts. Most of them seemed to be star-maps of various regions of the galaxy, but one was a diagram of the Solar System with all the planets depicted in their orbits. Hammond picked up a pencil and hastily drew a small picture on this chart. He drew a tiny rocket-propelled satellite speeding away from Earth, with the crude figure of a single man visible inside the sphere.

He pointed to the satellite and the little figure in it, and then pointed to himself. It did not seem to lessen the hostility of the crowd.

"How the devil can I tell them I slept in the satellite for centuries?" Hammond wondered groggily.

Then he saw that one of the charts depicted the northern constellations as seen from Earth, with the crossed lines of the celestial pole at the star Delta Cygni. He reached up and drew new crossed lines at the star Polaris. He pointed to that, then pointed again to the picture of the satellite leaving Earth and to himself. He hoped they would understand that he meant he had left Earth when Polaris was the pole star, but if they did not understand he did not know what else he could do.

Some of them understood at once. Jon Wilson, the leader, did. The hostility on his gaunt face faded into an expression of incredulity. He looked at Hammond and seemed about to voice his skepticism, but something in Hammond's appearance stayed him. There came into his deep eyes a hint of dawning awe.

"Do phrann?" he said. There was disbelief in his tone, but it was not violent, not sure.

He and the girl Iva and the others stared at Hammond, more startled now than suspicious. The man Lund spoke up with harsh denial strong in his attitude, and Quobba answered him loudly and excitedly, but Hammond did not care any longer what they said. The cumulative effects of his ordeal were closing down upon him and the whole room seemed to darken and move slowly around him.

Quobba ran toward him. He and the dark-haired girl supported Hammond. With Jon Wilson leading, they helped him down a corridor and into another room. This was a small sleeping chamber, cut from the solid rock like the other rooms of this strange underground refuge. Hammond was vaguely aware that they were stretching him out on a narrow bunk and covering him with something. Then sleep overwhelmed him.

A nightmare came to him. It seemed to him that he was not sleeping at all, but frozen and lifeless. With the strange duality of dreams, he looked and saw himself, Kirk Hammond, sitting in icy dignity inside a metal sphere as upon a throne. And the throne upon which this frozen Hammond

34

sat was far from Earth, moving out through the great darkness between the planets in vast and sweeping curves. The frozen eyes stared without seeing at planets and moons that rose up from the darkness and then fell behind him, and at the pallid glory of comets streaming light, and at the blaze and splendor of the distant stars. And then the fierce radiance of the sun fell upon those blind eyes as the throne-sphere he sat upon turned and came back. He was a king indeed of space and of time, for what was time to the dead? For year upon year, age upon age, he held his icy royal state and all was well until he heard a despairing voice say, *"Oh God, I could be bounded in a nutshell, and count myself a king of infinite space, were it not that I have bad dreams."* And then the nutshell-satellite crumbled away around him and he was alone in space and not a king at all but a dead man who must live again. And Hammond woke yelling aloud that line from *Hamlet* and fighting hands that tried to hold him down, until there was a sharp needle of pain in his arm and sleep came that had no dreams.

He half-awoke again, and again, and then there came a time when he awoke completely. He had a feeling that many days had passed. He was weak and limp but he no longer felt that sickening dizziness. He lay for some minutes, looking up at the smooth rock ceiling in which one bright globe shone softly. It had been no mere dream, then, that nightmare. It had been a deep memory carried by his physical body, the very texture of his being, of something his mind could not remember.

A whimpering dread came upon Hammond at the thought. He looked down at his hands and thought of those hands frozen and lifeless, resting on the arms of the ejection-chair while the satellite whirled him on its endless orbit until it fell into the gravitational field of Earth and was drawn down. Years, decades, centuries, piled one upon another, and how could a man go through all that and awake and still be human? How could he ever get the cold of space out of his bones, how could he keep the nightmare vision out of his soul? It would come again, and again, and he would go mad with it, and. . . .

He did not know that he was sitting up on the bunk and crying out until Quobba ran into the room, with the girl Iva close behind him. The blue man forced him back down with his big hands, speaking to him loudly and cheerfully as one might to a frightened child. Iva peered at him, startled and distressed.

Hammond quit struggling and lay back. He said dully, "All right, I'm okay." Then he realized that they could not understand, and forced himself to smile and nod his head.

They both looked relieved. Quobba said emphatically, "Ez nun do Vramen." He went to a corner of the room and brought back things he held up for Hammond to see, exhibiting them with the air of a defense attorney who has won his case.

Hammond recognized his own zipper-jacket and a few small things that had been in his pockets—a book of astrogational tables, a small slide-rule, a vial half full of the stimulant tablets that had been supposed to get him through the blast-off shocks more comfortably. Quobba grinned all across his massive face as he showed them, and Iva smiled at him too, though with a touch of awe in her clear dark eyes. And when Jon Wilson hurried in a minute later to inject something into Hammond's arm, he seemed reservedly friendly.

They believed him, Hammond realized. And suddenly he understood. Those simple objects—the textile fabric of the jacket, the book printed in a long-dead language, the other things, would be in this age relics of an ancient past. Everything about him, from the fillings in his teeth to the buttons on his pants, would be proof to a scientific mind. No words on his part could have been a tenth so effective in convincing them that he was what he claimed, and not one of their enemies the Vramen.

He thought he might as well make the point again, though, and he said "Vramen", and touched himself, and shook his head as vigorously as he could. Then he pointed to them and asked on a rising note, "Vramen?"

Iva shook her head fiercely, her blue-black hair brushing her shoulders. Her eyes flashed.

"Nun! Sin do Hoomen."

Hoomen? Was that what these people called themselves? It sounded very much like "human". He would have liked to learn more, but Iva pressed him back down on his pillow with firm hands. She spoke to him and he guessed that it was a command to sleep. He was afraid to sleep, afraid that the nightmare would come again and that he would be swept out through the dark in the cold loneliness of the dead. But he could not fight the drug that had been given him. He slept, and he did not dream.

Time passed, measurable to him only as sleeping and waking periods. In the waking times, he felt strength slowly returning to him. He had no appetite, and the rather insipid nutrient jellies they gave him were not such as to tempt one, but nevertheless he gained. He wanted to get up, but Jon Wilson and the girl Iva who was Wilson's daughter would not let him. Nor would they at first let him talk much, so that Hammond had little to do when awake but lie and look at the ceiling and think. He thought of friends dead for ages, of all the customs, languages, nations and races that had been his own world and that had now gone forever, and a terrible loneliness came over him. There were times when he felt that only one thing held him back from madness.

That thing was his curiosity. He wanted desperately to know more about this strange future Earth into which he had been catapulted. He wanted to know who the Vramen were and who these Hoomen were and why they hid, and what they were doing down here, and why some of them had the look of men never born on Earth. He wanted to know, especially, if that had been a space-ship that he had seen climbing the night on wings of thunder. He wanted to know everything about everything and there was only one way to know and that was to learn the language of these people.

37

Iva spent long hours teaching him, when he was able to sit up. She worked with pictures and gestures, building up his vocabulary patiently. There were a few haunting resemblances to the languages of his own time and general structure seemed the same, and that helped. But Quobba and the little yellow man Tammas helped not at all. It seemed that they talked a different dialect or used some form of slang, and finally Iva forbade them to teach him words.

But when Hammond was able to frame simple questions to Iva, he found they got him nowhere. She only looked uncomfortable and said, "My father will tell you."

"When?" he demanded. "How soon?"

"Soon," she evaded. "You can not speak well enough yet. You need more words."

It tantalized Hammond's curiosity. He was here in a world that appeared to be totally changed from the one he knew, and yet the simple barrier of language kept him ignorant of what it might hold. He felt like swearing.

Two sleep-periods later he lost all patience and demanded to be let out of his underground cell.

"I want some sun," he said. "I want to go out."

Iva looked grave. "Wait," she said, and left the room. She did not come back. Jon Wilson came instead.

He stood looking down at Hammond, and Hammond again got that chilling feeling that it was old John Brown of Pottawatamie whose deep eyes inspected him. He had a conviction that this was a man to whom ideas were important and that he would not hesitate to sacrifice any man, least of all himself, to an idea.

"You cannot go out yet," he said. "You are fortunate to be living. For a time, we did not think you would survive."

Hammond asked, "How long—" And then he stopped, his mind and tongue unable to frame the question.

How long was I dead? How many centuries did my frozen body ride through the darkness and the silence?

How could a man ask such a question? But Jon Wilson understood. He said,

"All the physical evidence of your body and your possessions puts your origin in a remote period. By the old chronology, the 20th or 21st Century."

"I was born in the year nineteen forty-nine," whispered Hammond.

Wilson thought for a moment. "Then by that chronology, though we no longer use it, this would be the year twelve thousand oh-nine-four."

Then it was true, and the star-clock had not lied, but still it was a truth too vast and terrible for Hammond to accept. He fought against it.

"But how could I live again? I've heard of hypothermia experiments, but a thing like this—"

Wilson shrugged. "I can't give you all the science of this age in a few sentences. Most of the terms, the words, you would not even understand. But—we found long ago in the first days of the conquest of space that a man stricken suddenly into deep hypothermia by the cold of space could be revived. Ordinary cold, ordinary freezing, shuts off circulation of blood to the brain so there is damage to the delicate brain cells before the full hypothermia can take hold. The cold of space freezes even the brain cells rigid before any damage can take place. The heart stops, everything stops, but without any ventricular fibrillation or cellular impairment. It was learned that the gradual application of heat to a body frozen in this way would in most cases start up the vital processes again."

Jon Wilson paused and gave Hammond a thoughtful glance. "In the old days they would have said that you were singled out by Providence. For in falling back into Earth's atmosphere in the satellite, the increasing warmth of frictional heating closely approximated the necessary curve of thermo-revival that brings a man out of deep hypothermia."

Hammond put his head between his hands and shut his eyes. Then after a moment he took refuge from this staggering revelation in a side issue.

39

"You said, 'Long ago in the first days of the conquest of space'. Then space is conquered?"

"Yes," said Wilson.

"The stars, even?"

"Yes."

"Then Quobba, and Tammas—"

"Quobba was born on one of the worlds of Vega. Tammas comes from Mizar. The men of Earth have colonized some far worlds since your day, Hammond."

Hammond felt a heavy leaping of his pulses. Then the dream of his own time had come true and the first fore-doomed little attempts like his own had been followed up, and the oceans of space were open to all men.

He said that, and Jon Wilson laughed. It was a harsh and shocking sound, and Hammond saw a deep hot spark in the man's eyes.

"Oh, no," said Wilson. "You're wrong. Space was con-quered, by men like you and by men like my own ancestors. But it does not belong to us, not to you nor to me and mine. Space belongs to the Vramen."

Hammond said, "Who are the Vramen?"

"They're why you can't go out," said Wilson. "They're our enemies, and they're your enemies too. They're still hunting over this whole coast. Their radar installations would have caught your satellite as it fell back to Earth and their fliers must have found your parachute in the sea. They're hunting for *you*, Hammond."

Chapter 5

HAMMOND LAY unsleeping, still stunned by the impact of a thousand centuries. It was the middle of the night, though in these rock catacombs one knew it only because the ceiling bulbs were dimmed and the murmur of activity from the other chambers quieted. He lay in the dimness and the silence, his mind feverishly going over all that Wilson had told him, and he felt all the vast events of those ten thousand years thunder down on him like an avalanche.

Jon Wilson had talked a great deal. For the first time he had answered fully and carefully every question Hammond put to him. Now Wilson slept because all this was old familiar stuff to him, the norm, the *status quo*. But Hammond could not sleep. His brain was a bright kaleidoscope and the visions evoked by Wilson's words went round in it, and round again until he was dizzy with them.

Fantastic, splendid visions. Earth sending out her ships and mourning them and stubbornly sending out more until one of them returned and the Big Step had been made— Someone, Hammond thought, was luckier than me—and then the ships going out proud and confident, taking the children of Earth to the empty planets and filling them with life, and after that like strong swimmers leaving the shallows of their youth behind, plunging into the black seas that run cold and tideless across the universe, girdling ten billion stars, until the children of Earth were spread across the galaxy. They were born now under the light of alien suns, on countless alien planets, and they had changed as Quobba and Tammas were changed to suit their environments, but still they were the children of Earth, and space belonged to them.

By every rule and right space belonged to them. Only they did not possess it. The Vramen did.

It was odd, Hammond thought, that already he was beginning to hate that name. He had never seen a Vramen. He had only a story Wilson had told him to go on, and for all he knew that story might be, if not exactly a pack of lies, at least so colored by fanatical prejudice as to be anything but true. He kept reminding himself how easy it would be for him to acquire a whole set of biases from these people simply because they had been good to him and he liked them, and because he had no other data by which to evaluate what they told him. Even the name they called themselves, *Hoomen,* was a semantic trap, aligning him automatically with them and against the non-human Vramen.

But no matter how judicious he tried to be about this, telling himself that he would reserve judgment on this or that point until he knew more about it, he could not help feeling a twinge of blind emotional hatred whenever he thought of the Vramen. Part of that, he knew, was transmitted to him from the intense feelings of everyone around him. But a good percentage of it was entirely his own, and he thought he knew why. It was because of space. He had taken his modest part in that conquest, he had given his life for it. And now that that life had been miraculously returned to him, it infuriated him to learn that a new, strange breed of man had sprung up as a direct result of that space-conquest and had pre-empted it, stepping arrogantly between human man and all he had worked for. Hammond had a very possessive feeling about space and space-flight. These had always been a personal dream and a personal challenge. And it was one of his personal tenets of faith that space ought to be just as free as it was wide.

The Vramen, according to Wilson, did not think so.

And who were these Vramen who arrogated to themselves the lordship of space? They were men and women of the same old Earth stock as the Hoomen, the ordinary humans. There was only one basic difference between them and ordinary humanity.

The Vramen did not die.

Hammond went over the story Wilson had told him for the hundredth time. It was an incredible story but he supposed that if an ancient Roman had awakened back in his own Twentieth Century he would have found atomic energy just as incredible.

The Vramen had happened, it seemed, more or less by accident. Some two thousand years before, while Hammond in his satellite was an unnoticed fleck of meteoric debris engrossed in his blind cold journey to nowhere, some scientists were exploring a region called the Trifid that was located in the densest, least-known part of the galaxy. It was a vast region of double and multiple stars involved in far-flung nebulosity, which Twentieth Century astronomers had called the Trifid Nebula. And somewhere in the stellar wilderness of the Trifid, upon a world they had named Althar, they had found the secret of indefinitely prolonged life.

"What *kind* of a secret?" Hammond had demanded, half-skeptically. "What could do a thing like that?"

"It's generally believed," Wilson told him, "that they found on that world a deposit of super-radioactive matter with emanations unlike anything we know. Even you must realize the deep effects of radiation upon life. But we don't really know what they found."

Whatever it was there on Althar, it did confer indefinite life on the normal perishable organism. The Vramen were not impervious to injury, but they were to disease and age. Nobody knew how long a Vramen could live because nobody had known one to die of old age.

The first Vramen were the discoverers of that secret hidden in the Trifid. They had enlarged their numbers by taking other carefully selected men and women in there to the mysterious world called Althar. When there were as many Vramen as they thought suitable, that was the end of it. No one else was allowed to go to Althar, or even into the Trifid. The mass of humanity remained as it had always been, most cruelly short-lived. The Vramen became a caste apart, living on and on.

"But is their super-longevity hereditary?" asked Hammond. "Do their children inherit it?"

"The Vramen have no children," Wilson answered. "Neither do they marry, in our sense, though I believe they have long companionships between themselves that may be matings."

Because all the Vramen were picked scientists, with no

arbitrary period put to their learning power, it had not been difficult for them to evade the disorganized attempts of the Hoomen first to force their secret out of them and then to destroy them out of sheer jealousy. They made themselves impregnable with powerful weapons and defenses, and then over the decades they began quietly to assume a background control over the whole galactic civilization. They did not take any official part in the government—the Federated Suns, Wilson had called it, a fine ringing phrase—but their scientific knowledge was so great and so constantly growing and their contributions to the general welfare so important that the Hoomen were grudgingly forced to submit to this shadowy dominance, granting to the Vramen through the council of the Federated Suns the one privilege they required—the privilege of keeping indirect control over all interstellar ships.

This was the one that set Hammond's back to bristling.

"According to the law," Wilson had explained to him, "every star-ship has a secret, tamper-proof device of the Vramen built into it. This can be used to explode the whole ship if it goes into the Trifid, which is closed to all but Vramen ships. Also, in every solar system there are Vramen stationed to keep constant radar check on every star-ship that comes or goes. That's why they're so hot after your craft, Hammond. They won't rest until they find it, and you."

Hammond found this a sufficiently disturbing thought. The one brush he had had with the Vramen power in the form of the hypno-amplifier, which would have forced him to give himself up like any suggestible imbecile if Quobba hadn't saved him, still frightened him to remember. And that, too, was part of his growing hatred of the Vramen. He had an old-fashioned ingrained notion that a man's mind, and the freedom thereof, was an inviolable right. In his own historical past some very great wars had been fought for the sake of that right. He was not prepared to surrender it meekly to these self-made supermen.

44

It was then that Wilson had dropped his final shattering bomb.

"There is one more thing I have to tell you, Hammond, and then you must make up your own mind what you want to do about it. To be brutally honest, you won't have a great deal of choice, but I would like to tell you as much as I can.

"You've been very curious about what we're doing down here in these dismal catacombs—why we're in hiding, afraid to show our heads above ground. It's very simple. We're engaged in an illegal activity, and if we're caught at it we'll get the extreme penalty."

He paused and then said quietly,

"We're building a star-ship."

Hammond stared at him. He did not know why he should have been so stunned by this revelation. Perhaps it was because the idea of a star-ship, legal or illegal, could still stun him.

"A star-ship?"

"Yes. It will not have the Vramen device in it. It will fly with a picked crew—all of us here are spacemen and volunteers—and it may eventually reach its destination."

Hammond's pulses began to hammer. He leaned forward. "Althar?"

"Althar. The hidden world of the Vramen. It's a suicide attempt, Hammond. We all know it." Wilson's eyes had that John Brown look again, ruthless and exalted. "But if we should succeed, we will have given all mankind indefinitely long life, freeing them forever from the tyranny of the Vramen and the vastly greater tyranny of time. We think it's worth the risk."

He stood up, looking down at Hammond.

"I don't know whether you will think so or not. We hope that you will join us. But that's a decision you must make yourself."

Hammond looked up at him incredulously. "Why would you want me? It doesn't make sense. Granted that all this is true, and I still can't half believe it, why me? I don't know star ships or stars. I don't know your technologies. I'm a primitive, compared to you people. What use would I be?"

"There's a big struggle ahead," Wilson said. "Even if we reach Althar and expose the Vramen's hoarded secret to the whole galaxy, that will only begin the fight. The peoples of the galaxy are used to the Vramen dominance and it will be hard for them to shake it off. And that's why we'll need you, Hammond. Once we prove to everyone you're what you are, one of the first of the oldtime spacemen, you'll become a symbol of the oldtime freedom of space we're trying to win back."

Hammond grunted. "I see. Propaganda value—I might have known."

"Don't decide now," Wilson had concluded. "Think it over. Talk to Quobba and Tammas and the others. Then decide."

Hammond was thinking it over now, lying awake and restless in the little dim rock-cut chamber. His head ached with thinking of it, but he had to decide what he wanted to do.

What did he want to do? He wanted to go back to his own time and the hell with all this crazy time and talk of starships and people that didn't die. No use thinking about that. He couldn't go back. He was in this time to stay and he had to make the best of it. But how was he to know what was best?

To begin with, Jon Wilson could be lying. These people might be no more than fugitive criminals hiding out from the law. No, he couldn't believe that. They were building something here, he had seen them at work. But even if it was a star-ship, that didn't prove that it was for any such far-fetched purpose as making a forbidden attempt to find the secret world of the Vramen. How could he be sure?

He groaned to himself. Why the devil had men ever gone to space anyway? They had really started something, back there in the Twentieth Century.

There was a heavy step and Quobba came into the little

room and bent over him, his big head outlined against the dim light.

"You feel bad?"

"I'm all right," Hammond said. He sat up. He asked, "Tell me, Quobba. Are you my nurse or my guard?"

The blue man shuffled his feet. "Well. Both, I guess."

"Meaning I'm still not trusted?"

"Not till we're sure you're with us. We're sure now you did drop out of the past, the way you said. But you could still turn against us and try to reach the Vramen."

"I see." Hammond thought for a moment, looking at Quobba. He felt that the big blue man was a fairly simple soul and would not be too good at deception. He said, "What do you think of the Vramen?"

Quobba said promptly, "They're——" The word he used meant nothing and Hammond said so. Quobba explained at length.

"So you think they're bastards," Hammond said. "Why?"

"Who wants to die?" Quobba asked reasonably. "Nobody. We wouldn't have to, if the Vramen would let us in on their secret. *They* keep right on living while we grow old and get weak and sick and die. They tell us, 'It's better for you not to live so long as us, you wouldn't like it and it wouldn't be good for you.' They say it's for our own good they won't tell us the secret. Our own good! That's a lot of—"

Here again he used a word that Hammond had not learned, but he thought he knew about what that word meant. And looking at Quobba it was impossible to believe that he was lying, so that meant that at least part of what Jon Wilson had told him was true. It came to Hammond that these Vramen really grabbed in a big way, if they had monopolized both the control of space and the secret of indefinite life.

Quobba had sat down on the corner of the bunk, which creaked under his massive weight. Looking at him, Hammond asked suddenly,

"You're really from Vega?"

47

The blue man seemed surprised by the question. "Sure. Vega Four."

"What's it like?"

Quobba shrugged. "A nice world. Different, of course—I've never yet really got used to yellow or red sunlight, or green grass, or things like that. I was a fool to leave it but I went space-crazy. Followed the ships for ten years, and then Shau and I got acquainted with Jon Wilson and decided to follow him."

Hammond tried to imagine what it would have been like to be born on the world of a blue sun, and to spend one's life along the starways. It was hard to imagine. And yet—he felt a small thrill of pride when he thought about it—he had helped pioneer the way to all this, long ago.

And his pride increased as he talked to Rab Quobba in these dim night hours, of the starways and the men who followed them. His head spun with the Vegan's tales of spaceman's life, tales of the vast glooms of cosmic clouds that ships rarely dared to enter, of wrecks and castaways in the vast unexplored fringes of the galaxy, of the strange autochthonous races that colonizing Earthmen had found on faraway worlds when they first landed. The thinking rocks of Rigel Two and the amphibious cities of Arcturus' inmost watery world, the uncanny tree-wizards of Algol Nine, and more information floating through Quobba's casual talk. Hammond was unable to tell which of them were fact and which were mere spaceman's legend, but through them all came the sense of the vast galactic web of commerce and travel in this latter age. And he, Hammond, who so long ago had dreamed of being the first man to go out around Earth's little moon, might voyage instead to the shores of the universe.

But there were the Vramen. Always they came back into Quobba's stories, and the Vramen had not let a ship go this way, or the Vramen had ordered shipping to go that way, until Hammond got the feeling of what it was like to have a superior caste over you, a super-long-lived oligarchy who held

48

the starways as their rightful realm, and to whom the passing human generations, the Hoomen, were mere ephemerae. Hammond began to share Quobba's detestation of the Vramen quite fully.

Next morning when Jon Wilson came, Hammond told him, "I'm with you, if all you've told me is true."

Wilson said gravely, "It is true. But before I can welcome you as one of us, the others must approve. Until then, please stay here."

When Iva Wilson came a little later, bringing a breakfast of the insipid nutrient jellies that Hammond had come to hate, he looked at her quizzically. "Are you my guard too, Iva?"

"Of course not," she said. "I never did believe you were a Vramen spy. I told Gurth Lund that first night that the Vramen would never use such a weak, helpless person as a spy."

Hammond laughed—the first time for how many ages?— and the dark-haired girl flushed quickly.

"Oh, I didn't mean it that way. You couldn't help being weak after all you went through."

After a little while Quobba came along and grinned at Hammond. "Well, you've just put your neck in it. Come along."

Hammond went with the Vegan, with Iva following them, to the small rock room that was Jon Wilson's study and the heart of the underground project. The Hooman leader was there with Lund, the sandy-haired man Hammond well remembered, and two other men.

Lund came forward promptly with his hand extended and with all hostility gone from his square young face.

"You've been accepted and that settles everything," he told Hammond bluntly. "I hope you don't hold my caution against me?"

"Of course not," Hammond said, and added, "If anyone had dropped in on me with a story like the one I told, I wouldn't have believed it either."

"So you become one of us," Jon Wilson said to Hammond. "I can't help thinking that it is fate that sent you to us so strangely from the past, as though you had been saved until just this time when you might be the most useful."

Lund said, "Of course we needn't warn you that you'll share our punishment if we fail."

"You mean the Vramen will kill us if we're caught?" Hammond asked.

Wilson answered him. "The Vramen hold no official position. Their domination is through their scientific prestige. They would turn us over to the nearest court of the Federated Suns, which would have to sentence us for breaking the starship laws."

He and Lund took Hammond through the workshops, showing him the amazing activity that was going on. After venturing a few questions, Hammond gave up asking and merely stared and listened. He had not the technical vocabulary yet, let alone the technical knowledge, to understand a tenth of what he saw. He was able to gather that atomic energy was the power-source for all the work down here, but the shielded machinery he saw was no more comprehensible to him than a radio would have been to a Hottentot.

He had supposed he would see the framework of a starship and he was eager for that sight. But the project was not that far along yet. The ship was being built in small sub-assemblies. Metal was secured from deep workings below the cavern refuge, the site having been chosen for that reason. When it was time to assemble the ship, the walls of the different chambers would be cut away carefully by some agency or energy that was not explained, and all would be converted into one large underground hangar.

"And when the ship is ready to go, we will simply cut away the rock roof and take off by night," Jon Wilson added.

"But won't the Vramen radar in Rurooma pick you up?" Hammond asked.

Gurth Lund said, "That's taken care of. We'll arrange to sabotage a legitimate ship and take off on its time. The

Vramen won't suspect anything until we're in deep space—on our way to the Trifid and Althar."

Jon Wilson's deep eyes shone. "For the first time in ages, a free ship will fly space again—a ship that the Vramen can't destroy with a touch."

Hammond met all the members of the band. There were thirty-two men and thirteen women and all of them were technicians or space-men carefully chosen for a definite part in the project. Beside Quobba and Tammas, who had gone on duty in the lookout, there were four natives of other star-systems—two red-skinned engineers from Betelgeuse, a swarthy little pilot from Altair, and a hollow-eyed, gray-skinned and gloomy-looking technician of some sort from Algol. Hammond looked in a kind of unbelieving wonder at these men who were evidence of how far humankind had spread from Earth. It was only after a time that he noticed how all of them stared at him with even more interest and awe.

"To all of us," Wilson said, "you're rather incredible. The time from which you came is the dawn of history to us, and few records of it have survived at all."

They were interrupted by the hurried appearance of Shau Tammas. The little Mizarian had come down from the camouflaged lookout-post.

"Quobba's getting worried," he said. "There's a Vramen flier cruising overhead, and he thinks they may suspect our location."

Wilson's gaunt face became instantly anxious. "I don't see how they could. But I'll go up."

He and Lund started up the spiral stair with Tammas. Hammond was hungry for a look at the sky and he followed them, without anyone objecting. Looking back, he saw that the Hoomen were stopping work as the alarming report passed from one to another. They were beginning to gather in anxious little groups. Up in the room inside the fake boulder were Rab Quobba and another man. The lookout

51

was so small that Hammond had to squeeze against the pedestal of the telescope-like instrument to get in at all.

"Take a look at the way that flier keeps circling back over this area," said Quobba to Jon Wilson.

Wilson bent to one of the cleverly concealed peepholes. So did Lund. After a minute Hammond located another of the peepholes and peered through the lens of the tiny aperture.

The lens was cleverly designed to give a wide field of vision. It was a bright, sunny morning out on the rocky coast. He could see blue waves creaming into white against the distant beach. It all looked remarkably familiar to Hammond, very lovely, very peaceful.

Until he saw the Vramen flier.

It came suddenly into his field of vision, a long shimmering torpedo without wings or jets and partly transparent. It was flying slowly and rather low, in steadily tightening circles.

"They surely can't have found us," Wilson said. "Their spy-rays wouldn't penetrate our shield."

He sounded worried just the same, and Hammond understood why even if he did not understand much about spy-rays and shields. The Vramen flier was coming ever closer in its circlings. Finally it poised motionless in mid-air, only a few hundred feet above the masked look-out post. Wilson groaned.

"No doubt about it now. We've got to bring that flier down fast before they can call more Vramen here."

Rab Quobba's massive face flamed with excitement. "I'll bring it down. Open the ceiling, Tammas!"

With eager quickness the little Mizarian swung aside the movable section in the ceiling of the fake boulder. Quobba was already at the base of the telescope-instrument, and Hammond realized suddenly that the thing was a weapon.

Chapter 6

Quobba had jabbed switches and a low powerful drone was now coming from the base of the "telescope". He sighted swiftly and then pressed a button.

A little puff of shining vapor sprang silently up from the end of the tube. Hammond had just time to think that if this were indeed a weapon it was a singularly unimpressive one, and then he stopped thinking that very quickly. For as the little puff of vapor sped upward it almost instantly changed size and shape and ballooned into a whirling, shining vortex that got bigger by the split-second.

The Vramen flier made a sudden frantic dart away from there, but a shade too late. One arm of the glittering, expanding vortex touched the tail of the flier and that whole tail section melted into dust. The flier plunged earthward but the vortex spun on higher and higher, still glittering and growing. Hammond followed it with awed eyes until he saw it suddenly snap out of existence. Only then did he look at the Vramen flier. The craft crashed down onto the ground a hundred yards away from the lookout and rolled over and over until it fetched up with a loud impact against a massive boulder.

"Got him," said Quobba, his eyes hot with fierce excitement.

Wilson said, "Gurth—Rab—destroy all trace of that flier before others find it here."

He pushed open the concealed door in the side of the camouflaged lookout and ran out into the sunlight with Lund and Quobba close behind him. Hammond yielded to the impulse to follow and ran after them.

His legs were a little shaky under him but the sun was a

welcoming brightness in his eyes and the wind from the sea was clean and cold in his face after the sterile conditioned air of the catacombs. He saw now that the whole front part of the torpedo-shaped flier was a crumpled wreck. Certain sections of the hull or fuselage were transparent and others were of opaque and silvery metal, and it came to him as a minor sharp surprise that in spite of that the hull was all of one piece, with some parts of its metal treated to make them transparent.

Quobba tore aside an unhinged door that now hung like a broken jaw. He squirmed into the interior of the wreck with Wilson and Lund after him, heading toward the wrecked forward part.

"They're dead—two of them!" the Vegan shouted.

Hammond, crawling in after them, glimpsed beyond their shoulders two men pinned and crushed and almost hidden by crumpled metal plates and stanchions. He was scrambling to follow them forward for a better look when he heard a slight sound behind him.

He turned, and then gaped like a fool. Back in the shadowy opaque mid-section of the flier, a figure was moving, rising from the floor. This was no man but a woman, for he glimpsed a mop of ashen-blonde hair and the curve of a white knee as she got unsteadily off the floor. She was young, and she wore the same costume of shirt and shorts as did the Hoomen women.

Wide blue eyes still stunned by shock stared at Hammond and at the Hoomen beyond him. He thought that her face, even now when it was blank and dazed, was one of the most beautiful he had ever seen, and one of the strongest. To Hammond, the strength detracted from the beauty. He resented the woman because he felt instantly that in many ways she was his superior, and always would be.

The moment endured, with Hammond staring wonderingly and the woman's eyes looking back with pain and shock in them, until Lund happened to look around. At first he saw only Hammond.

"What are you doing here?" he said angrily. "Get back to the—" He did not finish. There was an instant of complete silence and then Lund said two words. "Thayn Marden."

That brought Wilson's head around with a snap.

"Marden! Get her, Lund—don't hurt her—*look out!*"

The final words were a sharp warning and the men behind Hammond came scrambling desperately along the broken metal flooring toward him. Lund's voice seemed to have brought the Vramen woman suddenly out of her daze. She sprang toward a locker in the wall and clawed at its door. The door was jammed and would not open.

The agonized warning from Wilson made Hammond understand that there was danger. Whatever the woman was trying to get out of that locker would not be good for any of them. He was much the nearest to her. He sprang awkwardly and grabbed her. The next moment Hammond felt as though he had tackled a wildcat. The physical strength in this supple female body was so unexpectedly great, and he himself still so weakened, that his grip on her was almost broken. He hung on, his face pressed against her perfumed blonde hair, the two of them locked like lovers in a fierce embrace until Quobba reached them and grabbed the woman in his massive arms.

"Tie her hands," Wilson said. "Quickly, quickly!"

Lund tore a thin cable loose from the wreckage inside the flier and used the insulated wire to pinion her wrists. Hammond stood panting and shaken. The woman ceased to struggle when her wrists were bound but her blue eyes blazed with fury and indignation. She did not say anything.

"Take her to the lookout," Wilson said to Quobba. "Gurth and I will fuse the power-chambers." He added angrily to Hammond, "Go with them—get out of here!"

Quobba picked up the captive woman like a child and scrambled out of the wreck into the sunlight. Hammond went after him. The blue man hastened across the stretch of rock to the fake boulder. When they entered it Iva Wilson was there anxiously waiting for them. She looked at the Vramen woman in sheer astonishment.

"Thayn Marden!" she said.

"You know her?" asked Hammond.

Iva nodded. "Of course. She's been one of the Vramen at Rurooma since long before I was born."

That shocked Hammond profoundly. In the excitement he had forgotten how long-lived the Vramen were supposed to be. Now, looking at this woman they called Thayn Marden, the claim seemed preposterous. Her striking, clear-cut beauty had about it that unselfconscious quality of power and superiority that still made him bristle. But physically she looked no older than Iva.

Thayn had recovered all her poise. She stood arrow-straight and she looked at them, Hammond thought resentfully, as an outraged adult might look at vicious juvenile delinquents. And still she would not speak.

"There goes the wreck!" exclaimed Shau Tammas gleefully.

Hammond, turning to look out, saw that Jon Wilson and Lund had come out of the wrecked flier and taken shelter behind a big boulder some distance away. Inside the wrecked craft there shone now an intensely white point of light, and this spark grew in seconds into a slow, soundless explosion of light and force which enveloped the whole wreck. When Hammond's dazzled eyes regained vision, the wreck was totally gone and there was only a blackened patch of sand. Lund and Wilson ran to this and smoothed fresh sand over the scorched area. Then, smoothing away all footprints behind them, they hurried back into the shelter of the lookout.

Wilson, breathing hard, closed the door of the lookout. He ignored Thayn Marden. He went to one of the lensed loopholes and looked out.

"If they got off a message to Rurooma before they were shot down, there'll be other Vramen here in a few minutes. We'll wait and see."

They waited.

The minutes went by. In the close, stuffy little room where too many of them were crowded, no one spoke. Finally Wilson said,

"Nothing. They got no message off."

Quobba, still holding the Vramen woman by the arm, breathed a noisy sigh of relief.

Wilson came and stood in front of Hammond, and his face was made of planes as harsh as rock. He said,

"Why did you follow us out there? I told Gurth and Quobba only to come with me."

A spark of temper flared in Hammond. "I wanted to come. And it's a good thing for you I did."

Wilson looked at him dourly. "You were right, you *are* a primitive. But understand this—no matter how anarchic a time you came from, in this time you obey orders if you're one of us."

Hammond felt a hot resentment but he kept it to himself. Wilson turned toward the Vramen woman, and it was only then that Hammond noticed that the anger had momentarily left the woman's face. She had been keenly observing the exchange between him and Wilson and she was still staring at him as though fascinated.

Now for the first time she spoke.

"Who is that?" she asked Wilson, her eyes still on Hammond.

"Your people will find out," Wilson told her grimly. "The whole galaxy will find out before long."

"What do you mean, the time he came from?"

Wilson ignored that. "I have a question for you, Marden. How did you locate our refuge, which is completely shielded from spy-rays?"

Thayn Marden looked at him in scornful silence.

"Perhaps," said Lund thoughtfully, "the very fact of an underground area completely impenetrable to spy-rays gave her the clue."

Wilson said stubbornly, "Our ray-shield was arranged to make it seem a natural deposit of resistant metals."

Lund nodded. "And it would fool most of the Vramen. It did. But remember that Marden is one of the highest-ranking Vramen scientists in this System. She could guess the truth where another wouldn't."

Hammond, standing back with Iva against the wall of the crowded lookout room, only partly understood this talk of spy-rays and shields. He was less interested in it than he was in the woman herself. She was the first of the hated Vramen he had seen, and he thought he could understand now why they were so hated. You would get tired indeed of sharing the world and the Solar System and the whole galaxy with people who looked at you in the way this woman looked at the Hoomen, not a look of contempt so much as one of utter impatience with stupidity.

The odd thing was that when she glanced at Hammond himself, as she did several times while Lund and Wilson were talking, her expression was one of intense interest. Those brilliant blue eyes seemed to be trying to look right through him, and not quite succeeding. He realized that she was intrigued by him, not in any personal way at all but as a problem she could not yet solve.

Wilson pointed to the stair and said curtly, "Down there, Marden."

"You might as well stop this nonsense and come with me to Rurooma," she said. "You know it won't be long before others come to look for me."

"They're not all as clever as you," Jon Wilson said. "And—we now have you as a hostage. Go on."

The hatred in his deep eyes was mirrored in the faces of the others. Lund's face, in particular, was deadly as he looked at the Vramen woman.

Thayn shrugged and started down the little stair. They followed, leaving Tammas and another man on guard in the lookout. When he got down into the underground halls, Hammond saw the blazing excitement of the other Hooman men and women at this capture. They stared in mixed awe and hatred at the captive. Wilson explained briefly to them,

58

then led the way toward the small chamber from which he directed activities. Thayn's cool blue eyes missed no detail of the machines and labor in the rooms through which they went. And the astronomical charts upon the walls of Wilson's room instantly attracted her attention.

"So this is why you left Rurooma and hid here," she said. "You're attempting to build an illegal star-ship."

"Not attempting," Wilson said. "We're doing it."

Thayn frowned. "But you've only begun. This can't be the illegal ship we tracked on radar some time ago. You have another ship."

Wilson pointed to Hammond. "It was his craft you tracked. Do you want to know where it came from?"

"Yes."

Wilson told her. The telling took quite a few minutes and in that time Hammond felt the Vramen woman's eyes searching every detail of his appearance. But her face showed only complete incredulity as Wilson finished.

"I don't know what part of your conspiracy this man represents," she said, "but it's a foolish hoax."

"No hoax, Marden," said Wilson. "You know all about hypothermia. He really comes from that time. Every bit of evidence about him proves it."

"How would you know?" retorted Thayn. "Even we know little about that remote age. And what would a man of that time be doing with you outlaws?"

"He's one of us now," Wilson said. "And when our ship is built he'll go with us to the Trifid, to Althar."

There was a moment of silence. Thayn's face did not change but it seemed to Hammond that it hid a deep and powerful emotion.

"No," she said finally, in a low voice. "Oh, no, you will never go to Althar."

"But we will," said Wilson quietly. "And whatever the secret of life may be that you have hidden there, we'll find it. For ourselves, and for all Hoomen."

"You are children," whispered Thayn. "You talk of things

59

you do not know. If you knew what really lies at Althar—"

"*You* know," said Wilson. "That's why you're valuable to us. When our ship goes there it will not have any detonator in it, which eliminates one danger. You will help to eliminate any others by telling us exactly what and where they are."

Thayn's blue eyes flashed. "I will tell you nothing. You should know the Vramen better than that."

Wilson's face was gaunt and somber, unyielding as iron. "You will tell, and what you tell will be the truth. You will tell it under the encephaloprobe."

Hammond did not understand the word at all, but the Vramen woman obviously did. Her face tightened. She said, "You don't have one."

"We can build one. There are workers from many fields among us, including two psycho-technicians. They are quite familiar with the encephaloprobe. And if you try to resist, then—"

"You can destroy my mind but you will learn nothing," Thayn said. She added bitterly, "The encephaloprobe itself is one of the things that Vramen science gave you."

Wilson ignored that. He said, "It will take some time to construct a 'probe. You have that long to reconsider your decision. Don't mistake me. The thing will be used on you—and if you try to resist it, what happens will be your own doing." He turned abruptly. "Quobba, lock her in the small empty storeroom at the end of the north corridor. And set a guard outside the door."

Kirk Hammond felt a vague oppression as he watched the Vramen woman led away. He went out into the corridor and looked after her and Quobba. Iva Wilson came out too, and he turned to her and asked,

"What did she mean, destroy her mind? What's this encephaloprobe they were talking about?"

"It's an instrument psycho-technicians use," Iva said, "It has a long name but that's what people call it. It reads brains."

Hammond looked at her incredulously.

"It's true," she said. "I'm not a scientist, but the 'probe is common knowledge. It scans the synaptic patterns of a living brain and translates them into coded symbols. Of course, it can't scan *everything* in a person's brain, but it can search out the things most deeply imprinted on his memory, his dominant emotions and attitudes."

"But—how would it destroy her mind?"

"If the subject resists the 'probe with all his will, it may wreck his main synapses and shatter his mind."

Hammond felt a thrill of horror. "It sounds ghastly. Surely your father wouldn't use such a thing?"

"Our lives, the fate of all Hoomen, may depend on this," Iva said. "Yes, he would use it." She looked challengingly at him and asked, "Is it because Thayn is so beautiful that you hate the idea?"

Hammond smiled.

"She is beautiful. But she's not human like us at all," Iva said. "The Vramen are loveless and childless, caring only for knowledge and power. Don't be deceived by her beauty."

Hammond saw that Iva's face was flushed, her dark eyes brilliant with some strong emotion. "Why, Iva, you sound a little jealous," he said, and grinned.

She did not think it was funny. "If you think that," she snapped, "your wits must still be numb from your long sleep."

She turned sharply away and left him, but not before he had seen the hint of angry tears in her eyes. He looked after her, and then he shook his head and swore softly to himself.

Just before darkness fell on the upper world, Shau Tammas was relieved and came down from his hours in the lookout with disquieting information.

"Two Vramen fliers went up the coast an hour ago and then came back. They're already looking for Marden."

Jon Wilson nodded grimly. "Pass the order to everyone—and be sure they understand. No one, for any reason whatsoever, is to go out onto the surface."

Looking at them, Hammond felt a sudden cold doubt that

61

he knew these Hoomen at all. He had thought he knew them; in the long period of his recuperation and learning they had become familiar friends to him, people like the people of his own time. Jon Wilson seemed like many a stubborn upright man he had known in the old days, struggling indomitably for what he believed in. And yet Wilson was planning to do a thing to the Vramen woman that made Hammond wince back in repulsion.

Well, he had made his decision and it was right. He would go forward with the Hoomen and fight on their side. For the Vramen to own all space and dominate all its worlds was a wrong thing. Too many men, back even to his own Twentieth Century, had died to win space for that to be suffered! Yet Hammond felt now that though he had crossed the abyss of time physically, he was and always would be a stranger among these people, alone, lost forever out of his own world.

Chapter 7

THE UNEXPECTED happened four days later. During that time Hammond had felt a growing claustrophobia. He wanted to go outside. It was a frustrating thing to have returned as he had from the vastness of space, from the very coasts of death, and yet not to see anything of the world of this time except these rock chambers with their artificial light and sterile air. But Jon Wilson sternly forbade anyone to venture from the lookout.

"Vramen fliers are still searching this coast for Marden's craft," he said. "They don't give up easily. The search will go on for a long time."

"And in the meantime, what do I do?" Hammond demanded. "Everyone else here has work to do."

"There will be work for you, in plenty," said Wilson. "But not until you learn more. You can't even read our language, nor understand the symbols and settings of our machines. Learn."

So Hammond spent long hours with Iva and books. He liked the Hooman girl but he was too restless to enjoy the lessons. Between them, he roamed from the lookout, where he peered hungrily out at the sunshine and the stars, to the connected rock chambers where the endless work upon the star-ship sub-assemblies went on.

Two men had left their former work and begun a new task. One of them was an ordinary Hooman and the other, North Abel, was the Algolian, a tall man with a curious dull-gray complexion and a gloomy face. They were constructing a device that looked to Hammond like an incredibly complex form of electric chair. He learned that this was the encephaloprobe.

Looking at it with dislike, Hammond asked, "Is it true that the Vramen first invented this thing?"

"True enough," said Abel. "But they gave it to us freely. Why not? It's to their advantage. Our courts use it to test anyone suspected of plotting against the Vramen. There's never any error."

"But," Hammond objected, "Iva said that anyone who used all his will-power could resist this thing, even though it wrecked his mind. A determined man couldn't be questioned, then."

Abel snorted. "The Vramen don't give away all their inventions, Hammond. I hear you had a little experience with their hypno-amplifier? Well, using that, they can beat down any mental resistance to the 'probe."

"But you don't have that," Hammond said. "So—"

The Algolian shrugged. "So if Marden resists, it's liable to tear her brain apart. I hope not. This is a lot of work for nothing, if that happens."

His matter-of-fact callousness grated on Hammond, but he knew enough by now of the attitude of these people toward the Vramen that he did not protest. He too hoped that Thayn Marden would not resist. He didn't want to see anyone's mind rent to tatters. He hoped that she would talk her head off and that they would be able to finish the ship and get out of this hole in the rock, to Althar or anywhere else so long as it was not here.

It was then that Hammond got his surprise. He went to Jon Wilson to ask him if any progress had been made with the Vramen woman, but Wilson, who had been talking with Lund, forestalled him.

"I was going to send for you, Hammond. An odd thing has come up. Marden wants to talk to you."

Hammond stared. "With me? Why on Earth—"

Lund interrupted, saying uneasily, "I still don't like it. You know the Vramen. It's a trick of some kind."

"Possibly," Wilson said. "But she won't even talk to us. Hammond might be able to persuade her not to resist the encephaloprobe." He turned back to Hammond. "She's very interested in you. She thinks that your claim to be from the past is a hoax, but she's not quite sure. And she's eager to find out—all the Vramen are extremely interested in remote history. If you can convince her of your origin and get her to talking, you might be able to convince her that we're in dead earnest about using the encephaloprobe."

Hammond felt an odd little pulse of excitement. "But she may guess what I'm up to."

"Of course she'll guess it," Wilson said acidly. "The Vramen are a lot of things but they're not fools, not with all their many lifetimes of experience. Remember that."

The guard outside Thayn Marden's room had his instructions. He very carefully unlocked the door and let Hammond inside, and immediately shut the door after him.

A softly glowing ceiling bulb lit the bare little rock room. There was a cot and chair and little else. The Vramen woman had risen to her feet when he entered, and now she faced Hammond. She did not look like one of the superhuman lords of space he had heard so much about. She looked like

64

a remarkably handsome blonde young woman with intelligent blue eyes and a figure, as revealed by her brief white shorts, that ordinarily Hammond would have whistled at. He did not feel like whistling now. He felt a little scared.

Thayn made an easy gesture toward the chair. "You might sit down. And why do you stare at me like that?"

Hammond shrugged and sat down. "I don't know. I guess it's because I've never talked with an undying woman before."

Thayn made an angry, derisive sound. "Undying? The same old childish fairy-tale. Because we have longevity you Hoomen prattle about—" Then she broke off. "But I forgot. You're not supposed to be a Hooman at all, are you?"

"No, I'm not." He looked at her, fascinatedly. "How long-lived are you? How old are you?"

"A little more than two hundred years old," said Thayn.

It shook Hammond. For a moment his nerves bristled as though at the proximity of someone quite unhuman. His feeling must have shown in his face, for Thayn said,

"Why should you look like that? If your claim is true, you've been living for over ten thousand years."

"Not living," Hammond told her. "Not quite living."

"You remember nothing of all that time?" she asked skeptically.

I remember nothing but a dream. A dream of a man who sat in a tiny sphere like a king upon a throne, with frozen face and blind eyes turned upon the cold realms of space that he moved through forever and ever.

"Nothing," said Hammond, almost in a whisper.

Thayn's face changed. She was silent for a moment, looking at him keenly. She said in a different tone,

"You do not talk or look like an imposter."

"I wish to God I was one," said Hammond.

"Do you mind if I ask you some questions?"

"Go ahead."

She asked them. They were remarkably quick, searching, pointed inquiries concerning the Twentieth Century. Some

65

of them seemed to be more or less repetitious of ones already asked, and then it dawned on Hammond that she was cross-checking his answers very swiftly and scientifically. Especially, her questions dwelled on the first space-pioneering attempts.

When she stopped she looked sorely puzzled and increasingly excited.

"I can almost believe you *are* from that remote time," she said. "We Vramen have formed an hypothetical reconstruction of that dawn age, and no Hoomen know our researches. Yet your answers, with a few exceptions, check with ours. And the exceptions could be mistakes on our part."

"Hypothetical reconstruction?" repeated Hammond. "Don't you know from records what that age was like?"

She shook her head. "There are no records. The interplanetary wars of the Twenty-Third Century pretty well destroyed them, on Mars and Venus as well as on Earth."

"Interplanetary wars?" said Hammond. Then he said heavily, "That's fine. That's what we were working for, what we risked our lives for. The wonderful space age. Planet wars, and Vramen who own space, and people trying to get them off their necks. That's what our wonderful goddamned space age turned out to be."

Thayn looked at him, her blue eyes brilliant with excitement. "Either you are the cleverest imposter ever heard of, or your story is true. And it all checks—that parachute-device we found, like nothing made for ages—" She broke off, then said intently, "Listen, Kirk Hammond. Don't let yourself be involved in this Hooman plot. It will come to nothing, and you could get killed."

"This anxiety of yours about me is touching, but hardly convincing," Hammond said sourly.

Her eyes flashed with impatience. "Do you suppose I care what happens to you personally? You represent, if your story is true, a vast storehouse of knowledge of the remote past. I don't want that knowledge to perish."

Hammond could believe that, at least. And it gave him a

lead. So far, all the information had come from him but he attempted to reverse that now.

"There'll be no danger," he said lightly. "When our ship is completed, we'll go to Althar and find out how you Vramen make yourselves so long-lived."

"You haven't a chance in a billion of reaching Althar," she said. "We keep too close a watch on the whole Trifid. And even if you passed the Vramen—"

She stopped suddenly.

"Yes?" said Hammond.

Thayn shook her head. "Oh, no. They'll get no information from me, either by tricks or by the encephaloprobe."

"Not even to save your mind, your sanity?"

"No, not for that or anything," she answered, and her tone carried conviction to Hammond. "Their quest is quite hopeless, believe me. I can't help it if they're determined on suicide. But I do want to save you and all the knowledge you have from a useless death."

In her earnestness she laid her small hand on his wrist. Hammond flinched slightly and instantly Thayn's expression changed.

"So you've already picked up the Hooman hatred of us?" she said, her eyes searching his face. "You too think us unhuman?"

He tried to find words of denial, but Thayn turned away from him. She looked weary and dejected. And for the first time Hammond felt a spark of real sympathy for her.

"Are you really going to be so foolish as to let them wreck your mind?" he asked.

"I will tell nothing that will help Hoomen to reach Althar," she said, without turning.

"But they're—we're—going there anyway," Hammond said. "You might as well tell."

"Why should you care what happens to someone who is not human?" she said. And of a sudden she turned and came over and stood facing him, close to him. "Am I really so alien, so repulsive, in your eyes?"

67

She was looking up at him, and her tilted white face was provocative in its mock-innocence. The subtle perfume of her glimmering blonde hair made his pulses pound. There were little taunting devils in her eyes that utterly belied the softness of her face and voice. Her small hands reached out and grasped his shoulders, and her red lips were very close.

"Am I, Kirk Hammond?"

Hammond fully realized what she was doing. Yet for his life he could not refrain from the kiss she invited. Her half-parted lips were strangely cool and sweet, and her supple body was firm and elastic in his grasp. Next moment he was thrust violently away and Thayn was looking at him in scornful triumph.

"It seems I am not. But you are to me—I'd as lief be touched by an animal. By a dumb brute!"

Hammond, after a moment, said steadily, "All right, I hurt your feelings and you wanted to hurt mine. Are we even now?"

The scorn and anger left Thayn's face. She said, "You're right. I'm used to the hatred of the Hoomen, but you are of another age and your action hurt me. For a moment, I was small and spiteful."

The avowal was so honest that Hammond could not help admiring her. And the subtle scent of her hair was still in his nostrils.

He said, "I meant what I said, Thayn. I hate to see your mind destroyed."

"I cannot and will not help these people," she said. "Tell them so. And—come again if they will let you. I have much more to ask you about the old times."

The guard carefully let Hammond out of the little locked chamber. He had a lot to think about as he went through the busy work-chambers in search of Wilson.

Wilson listened intently when Hammond told him what Thayn had said about Althar. He repeated it slowly. " 'We keep too close a watch on the whole Trifid. And even if you passed the Vramen—' That seems to imply that there are

68

other obstacles for us at Althar, beside the Vramen. She added nothing to that?"

"Nothing. She stopped short as though she realized she was letting information slip out."

"The Vramen make very few slips," Wilson said skeptically. "Her 'information' could be quite calculated."

"I can talk to her again," Hammond suggested. "She seems quite eager to see me, now that she's practically convinced I'm what I say I am."

It was odd, he thought, how tensely he waited for Wilson's reply to that, as though a great deal depended upon it. He did not know quite why he should feel like that. But he did know that Wilson's answer, when it came, was a shock.

"North Abel says the encephaloprobe will be finished by tomorrow night. We'll use it on her the following morning, and it's her own fault if she resists it."

"But if she does, you learn nothing," Hammond said. "And if I *could* persuade her not to resist, you'll learn everything."

Wilson finally nodded. "You may as well try again to make her see reason. I'll tell the guard to let you in tomorrow afternoon."

He looked shrewdly at Hammond as he added, "You regard the encephaloprobe with horror, don't you? The necessity for it repels you?"

Hammond nodded. "I don't like to see even a Vramen's mind wrecked."

"Neither do I," Wilson said. "I'm not like Lund and some of the others, though they have good reason for their bitterness. But like it or not, with the future of all Hoomen hanging on this, the thing will be done. Try to make her realize that."

On the next afternoon when he entered the small prison-room, Hammond had his mind made up. He didn't know for sure whether he liked Thayn or detested her, but like Wilson he had no desire to see her mind blasted. He said so to her as earnestly as he could.

She shook her head. "I will not yield to the probe."

"Would it really be so terrible if other people, the ordinary Hooman men and women, had longevity too?" he demanded resentfully.

Thayn said, "Yes. It would be terrible."

"But why?"

"I can't tell you that. I will not tell it to anyone, not even under the probe."

Hammond felt helpless, and angry because he was helpless. "All right," he said roughly. "I hate to see this happen to anyone. But if you're determined to put caste loyalty ahead of your own sanity, there's nothing I can do about it."

Thayn did not answer that for a moment. Her clear eyes studied his face, and then she said,

"You don't want me made into a mindless idiot?"

"I told you, I don't want that to happen to anyone."

"You can prevent it if you wish," she said. And then as he started to object she added quickly, "No, I'm not suggesting that you help me escape. I know you wouldn't do that."

"Then what?"

She spoke very rapidly. "The encephaloprobe was a Vramen invention. We taught the Hoomen how to construct it, but they all follow our original plan, generating an ultra-high electromagnetic radiation capable of penetrating tissue and scanning the minute electric impulses of the human brain. The probe that has been built to use on me would have the same wiring diagram as every other."

Hammond stared at her uncomprehendingly. "So?"

Thayn said, "There is a small terminal board in the back of the instrument, inside the shield. It has twelve numbered binding-posts. It would be quite easy to change the whole wiring diagram. Wire Two should go to Post Four, Wire Four to Post Six, and Wire Six should be disconnected completely."

Hammond began to understand. "What would that do?"

"Change the quality of the 'probe's radiation. I could resist it then without having my mind wrecked."

70

Hammond got to his feet. "I've sided with the Hoomen in this fight. I believe in their cause, and I don't see why the Vramen should hog all space and long life. Now you're asking me to double-cross them."

"It amounts to that," Thayn admitted. "But they won't get the information they want from me in any case. This would merely save my mind. I could, you know, pretend mindlessness after they use the probe."

Hammond shook his head, feeling increasingly angry and upset. "No, I can't do it. I'm sorry they're going to do this thing to you, and I'm sorry you're so blind stiff-necked obstinate. But I'm not responsible for it."

Unexpectedly Thayn said, "You're right, it's not your responsibility. Well, I can't blame you. I only wish that when fate brought you from your past age, it had brought you to the Vramen instead of these Hoomen."

And of a sudden, she smiled. "Since nothing can be done about tomorrow, let us forget it. I want to hear more about that time when the first men went out from Earth. So long—so long ago."

The hours went by as she questioned him, and never once did she refer to what was to come. Only, when Hammond was about to leave, she came up to him and said,

"I think this is goodbye, Kirk Hammond. But I have one favor to ask, something that the Hoomen might do at your request."

"It's no good, Thayn," he said. "They're determined on this probing, and I can't talk them out of it."

"That's not what I meant," she said. "But after it's over—will you ask them to destroy my body? I've lived very long—but I have no desire to live on without a mind."

He did not know what to say to that. He looked at her, feeling a little sick, and then nodded, and turned and rapped for the guard to open the door.

That night Hammond could not sleep. He had made an appeal to Jon Wilson not to use the probe, and it had been rejected so sternly that he had known it was useless to carry the subject farther. He wondered if Thayn was sleeping. Somehow he felt sure she was, even though the morrow would end her mind, her personality.

He damned the fate that had brought him out of his own time to this crazy age. These people had scientific attainments far beyond those of his own time, they had conquered the stars. It was a pity that they, especially Thayn Marden, could not make more sense.

He washed his hands of the whole business. It was not his fault, any of it. Let it happen, he couldn't stop it. He would go to sleep.

He did not go to sleep.

After a while he rose quietly from his bunk and without putting on his shoes he walked stealthily out into the corridor.

"I'm a fool," he told himself.

All right, so he was a fool. He was the kind of a fool that couldn't let this nightmare happen.

He was with the Hoomen. He would not have let Thayn escape, to bring the Vramen down on his friends. But this business of reducing her to an idiot, without any gain whatever, was too much.

There was no one in the main laboratory and workshop rooms. The lights were dimmed and everyone slept except the watch on duty in the lookout above. Hammond made straight for the encephaloprobe. Thayn's description had been accurate. It took only a few moments to change the wires.

Hammond went back to bed and slept.

When he awoke the next morning he was surprised to find that he did not feel guilty. He felt relieved. He realized now how much the thing had weighed upon his mind.

"They're bringing Marden out now for the probing," Iva Wilson told him, a little later.

"You're not going to watch it?" Hammond asked.

Iva shook her head. Her face was pale. "I couldn't. I hate

72

the Vramen and I hate Marden, but this—even though it's necessary, I don't want to see it."

Hammond left her and went to the main laboratory. Few of the other Hoomen appeared to share Iva's feelings—they were nearly all there to watch.

Thayn came quietly with Lund and North Abel. Her glance fell casually on Hammond's face but she did not speak or nod.

"Your last warning, Marden," said Jon Wilson grimly. "Resist the probe, and what happens will be your own doing."

She made no answer. North Abel, a little uncertainly, gestured toward the seat around which the complicated apparatus of the probe was arranged. When Thayn silently sat down the Algolian looked relieved, as though he had feared a messy struggle to force her into it. She looked stonily ahead as the big metal helmet was placed carefully over her head. Her face, the only part of her head not covered by the helmet, was white and cold and expressionless.

"Don't resist. Relax," said Abel to her. And he repeated it, almost in a tone of entreaty. "Relax."

He went to the control panel and began turning switches. There was now a breathless silence on the part of the whole watching group. Into that silence stole a sound of droning power from the machine.

Abel carefully turned a rheostat. Thayn flinched slightly and suddenly closed her eyes.

"I'm starting," said Abel.

He touched a switch, and a roll of paper tape began to come clicking out of a slot at the side of the coding unit of the machine.

Hammond felt a sharp shock. Had he failed, was the woman getting the full blast of the probe? Her face was very white and strange and he might have got the wiring wrong and—

North Abel, bending over the tape, said suddenly in a puzzled voice, "I don't quite understand what I'm getting—"

Hammond exhaled a deep breath. Then he had not failed. Thayn was merely acting.

The guard came running down the spiral stair from the lookout, yelling, and every head turned toward him.

"Our radar in the lookout is picking up strong high-octave radiation that comes from down *here!*" he cried. "What are you doing?"

They stared at him, not believing.

"You must be wrong," Jon Wilson said. "There's no radiation down here high enough to get through our shield."

"I'm not wrong," said the man, "and you'd better find the leak and shut it off before every Vramen flier along the coast has it on radar."

Suddenly Gurth Lund ran forward shouting at North Abel. "Shut the 'probe off! Now!"

The Algolian, uncomprehending but obedient, reached out and turned the switches. The droning of the encephalo-probe died.

Thayn Marden opened her eyes.

"You said the probe wasn't working right," Lund said fiercely to Abel. "It's the only thing that could be leaking high radiation."

Abel shook his head emphatically. "Impossible. I wired and tested it myself."

A fatal foreknowledge came upon Hammond then, as though he heard the rumble and cracking of the rock roof falling in on him. He looked at Thayn and there was a sickness in him, and a shaking rage.

"Check it," said Wilson to North Abel.

Abel took off the back shield. He looked at the wiring and then up at them with a stricken face. "The wiring has been altered. Deliberately—to make a signal that would reach the Vramen radar."

All Hammond could do at that moment was to stand and glare at Thayn, and out of the helmet her face looked at him calmly.

"You—" he began, his voice choking.

74

Lund saw, and heard. "There's our traitor," he said, pointing at Hammond. "Look at him. I told you what would happen if you let Marden get hold of him. I told you—"

He plunged forward and caught Hammond by the throat.

Hammond fought him off and there was a roaring in his ears and a yelling of many voices around him and then it all stopped and everything was quiet. And in that quiet it seemed that a clear, cold voice spoke in Hammond's brain. It was like that strange mental voice that had spoken to him on the night when he and Quobba crouched beneath the boulder, hiding from the firefly ships.

"Put down your weapons, all of you," said the chill mental voice.

Hammond looked upward as Lund released him. Down the spiral stair from the lookout post a half-dozen men were coming. Two of them carried objects like bulky searchlights, from which sprang broad fans of pale force or light that enveloped every Hooman in the rock hall.

It was the weapon of hypnotic attack, the hypno-amplifiers. And as he realized that, Hammond realized also that neither he nor any of them were wearing the protective metal turbans now. He looked up at the calm faces and superb bodies of the descending men, and he looked at Thayn, and he heard Jon Wilson groan.

"The Vramen. This—"

No one said anything more. In Hammond's mind came another cold, hypnotic command.

"Sleep now!" it ordered. *"Sleep!"*

The Hoomen were already sinking to the floor around him as darkness swept over Hammond's brain.

Chapter 8

IT WAS with an unusual sensation of strength and vigor that Hammond awoke. For the first time since his strange resurrection in this future world he did not feel a dragging weakness. Rarely, indeed, had he ever felt so well.

He looked around him, puzzled. He was lying on a soft, low couch. At its foot stood an instrument like a tall lamp whose spiral glass bulb projected a flood of rosy light upon him. He wondered fleetingly if that was what had washed away his former weakness. Then the thought faded out of his mind as he looked past it at the room. It was small. Its floor, ceiling, and three of its walls were of a substance that looked like green porcelain. The fourth wall, a slightly curving one, was perfectly transparent and admitted the brilliant sunshine unhindered.

"Good God!" Hammond exclaimed, as memory suddenly rushed over him. "The Vramen—"

He remembered everything now, and the memory was a painful shock. Thayn had made a fool of him as easily as though he were a child. She had tricked him into altering the probe into a signal device that called the Vramen to the underground refuge. He could remember them using the hypno-amplifiers, the command to sleep, and now—this.

Hammond leaped to his feet and went to the single door of the room. It was locked, and all his hammering on it had no result. Baffled, he turned and went to that curved transparent wall which was actually a great window.

He looked forth, and was stunned.

He was high in a city. And it was such a city as neither Kirk Hammond nor any other man of his time had ever seen. This was no vast planless metropolis of huddled structures.

There were no more than a hundred buildings in this city. But they were the buildings of giants, colossal pylons, each one almost a mile in height. Each gigantic pylon looked like an erect bundle of round glass rods, the cross-section being such as to admit maximum sunlight to the interiors. Flashing and glittering in the sunshine, with sleek fliers flitting to and fro above them, the pylons were mind-rocking.

"Rurooma," Hammond whispered. "The city Rurooma, as the Hoomen described it. And that means—"

His presence here meant tragedy. It meant that he and all his Hooman friends, overpowered by the Vramen, had been brought here to be punished for their conspiracy.

Hammond felt the anguish of guilt. It was a bitter irony that he, who had sympathized so deeply with the Hooman aspiration to make space free again, should have been the one to bring ruin to their hopes. Where were Jon Wilson and Iva and the others now?

He swung around sharply as the door opened. When he saw that it was Thayn Marden, a hot, bursting anger made him start toward her with his hands clenched.

Thayn spoke quickly but calmly, displaying a small plastic tube she held.

"I can shock you unconscious with this if you force me to."

Hammond stopped, shaking with rage. Yet even in his fury he admitted to himself that the Vramen woman was more beautiful than ever. She now wore shirt and shorts of a black, silky material that made the loveliness of her supple white body transcendant. On her breast was an odd badge of glittering gems, and there was a jewelled band around her blonde hair. Her face was quite calm, her blue eyes inspecting Hammond gravely.

"What have you done with Jon Wilson, and Quobba, and the others?" he demanded savagely.

Thayn said unhesitatingly, "They're all right. Like you, they've been kept here the last four days, awaiting trial."

"Four days?" Hammond repeated, for the moment astonished out of his anger. "Do you mean it's been that long?"

Thayn nodded. "When our medico-technicians examined you, they found your body still suffering from that long deep hypothermia. They recommended keeping you under therapeutic radiation during this time."

Hammond's mind reverted to her statement about his friends. "You say Wilson and the others are all right. How do I know you're not lying?"

"We Vramen are not in the habit of lying."

"I suppose it wasn't a lying trick you used on me?"

"I told you that if you altered the wiring of the encephaloprobe my mind would be unharmed. That was the truth, wasn't it?"

"You didn't tell me I was signalling your friends," he said bitterly. "It amounted to a lie."

Again, Thayn Marden displayed an unexpected honesty. "Yes, it did," she admitted. "However, it was a case of extreme emergency. Any means is excusable to prevent Hoomen from going to Althar."

"You deliberately played on my sympathy for you," Hammond said. "No decent human woman would use a trick like that. But it would come naturally enough to a woman who isn't really a woman, a two-hundred-year-old creature without real emotions."

He wanted fiercely to hurt her and he succeeded. Thayn winced, and when she spoke again after a moment her voice was dull with pain.

"You have a right to say that." She looked at him steadily. "But now that you have said it, will you hear why I've come?"

"To tell me that I'm to be tried and punished with the others?" he said. "All right. I'm ready."

"You will not receive punishment unless you're utterly intractable," Thayn said. "You've been examined most carefully in our laboratories, during your sleep. We know now that your story of coming from the remote past is true, for we scanned your mind with the encephaloprobe."

78

Hammond felt a sense of outrage. "You used that damned thing on *me?*"

"It's always used on accused persons before trial," Thayn said. "A Vramen psycho-technician with a hypno-amplifier sees to it that there is no resistance."

"I hope you enjoyed learning how I feel about the Vramen."

"We found out many things. But the 'probe can't search out everything in a man's mind, only dominant memories and emotions. We got tantalizing fragments, glimpses of your remote time of which—as I told you—no other record remains."

She came closer and spoke very earnestly. "You could add tremendously to our knowledge of that dawn of the space age. If you agree to help our researches, to cooperate fully with our historians and psycho-technicians, we'll ask the Hooman court to suspend sentence on you for your part in the conspiracy."

"No deal," Hammond snapped. "I'll do nothing for you and your little caste of supermen. I stick with Wilson and my friends."

"That's because you don't know the truth," Thayn said. "They're jealous of the Vramen and they've infected you with their jealousy. They hate us, and yet the truth is that the Vramen have never harmed humanity in a single way, but have helped them in many."

"If you want to help humanity, why not let them all have the same long lives as yourselves? Or would that be helping them too much?"

Thayn looked a little weary. "I see that you won't listen to reason. You've learned the Hooman prejudices. And you're resentful of me especially because you're in love with me."

"In love with—" Hammond stared at her blankly, and then said, "For God's sake, you really believe that, don't you? What gave you that crazy idea—the fact that I felt sorry for you?"

Thayn smiled. "I told you the encephaloprobe records

dominant memories and emotions. I went over all the records, and yours clearly indicates that you've been in love with me since you first saw me, though your prejudice against Vramen has made you crowd the feeling down into your subconscious."

And before Hammond could say any of the things he wanted to say Thayn turned and went out of the room.

Hammond swore in frustration and anger. That, he thought, was how much their brain-probing was worth. He had felt Thayn's physical attraction, any man would feel it. And she, unhuman herself and therefore unable to distinguish between human emotions, had taken that as evidence that he was in love with her. In love with a two-hundred-year-old Vramen woman! He laughed.

An hour later the door was opened and two men entered. They were clean-cut young men in black uniforms with an emblem of clustered golden disks. Hammond knew from what Quobba had said that it was the insigne of the Federated Suns government. And since Vramen had no official part in the government, these must be Hoomen.

One of them said quietly, "Please come. We are to take you to your trial."

Neither of them wore a visible weapon, but he had no doubt that they had them. He shrugged and went with them.

The corridor outside was wide and curved, its walls and ceilings of a substance like cool green glass somehow lighted from within. There was a small crowd there—a half-dozen other uniformed men, and all the men and women of Jon Wilson's band, with Rab Quobba's massive head towering above everyone. Hammond went to them.

"Wilson—Iva—you're all right? I was afraid—"

The words trailed into silence. Jon Wilson was looking at him with a stony hostility. Gurth Lund looked as though he wanted to kill him. Even Quobba and little Tammas avoided his gaze and Iva stared unhappily at the floor.

"Look," said Hammond. "I know what you're thinking. I don't blame you for feeling that way. But please—"

A guard officer came up to him. "You can't talk here. The court is waiting."

They were marched quietly along the corridor and into a small metal room that proved to be a lift which went suddenly downward with breathtaking speed. Hammond found himself beside Iva Wilson.

"Iva, don't they realize that Thayn Marden tricked me, that I didn't do it purposely?"

She glanced at him briefly, then away again. "They say you did do it deliberately—that you betrayed us all for Thayn."

The lift stopped and they were led from it into a large and austerely beautiful hall. Its floor was a lake of smooth black. The walls just above the floor were dusky gray, and this shaded upward through lighter and lighter grays to the pure white climax of the vaulted ceiling. There was a large audience of men and women in the place, sitting in semicircular rows. Upon a dais facing them sat a man wearing the clustered-suns emblem, and on the wall above his head glittered a large replica of the insigne of the Federated Suns. Hammond saw no jury, no provision for attorneys, nothing else like a Twentieth Century court. He did see, on one of the front seats, Thayn Marden sitting with three men who wore the same curious badge she did.

"The damned Vramen are here to see that we get our proper punishment," he heard Rab Quobba mutter to Tammas.

As Hammond and his fellow prisoners were led to stand directly under the dais of the judge, he heard a murmur of voices from the spectators and became suddenly aware that everyone was looking at him. Apparently news of his strange history had spread. Even the Hooman judge, a stern-faced, middle-aged man, examined him with a keen and particular interest. Then he spoke to them all.

"You are charged with the offense of attempting to con-

81

struct an illegal star-ship. During this activity and as a direct result of it, you caused the deaths of two Vramen, whose patrol flier you destroyed by means of a vortice-gun, an illegal weapon. You further put under restraint and threatened with extreme injury a third Vramen." He picked up a sheaf of papers. "These are the official encephaloprobe records of your minds. You have had a chance to examine them. Do you protest any part of these records?"

Jon Wilson, bitter-eyed, said, "We will not protest the records."

The judge looked at Thayn. "Thayn Marden, as the person bringing the charge against the accused, you also have been permitted to examine the records. Do you protest any part of them?"

"I do not," Thayn answered.

It became apparent to Hammond from the speed with which all this was carried through that it was a mere legal formality, that no one expected the encephaloprobe's findings to be challenged. How could you challenge a precise, scientific recording of a man's mind? In this super-modern court there was no place for lawyers and legal tricks.

The judge was speaking again to the prisoners. "You knew that you were breaking a basic law of the Federated Suns when you attempted to build an unauthorized star-ship. You know that this government long ago entered into an agreement with the Vramen providing that no star-ship would be built or licensed without the incorporation into it of their Restrictive Control device."

Wilson answered that, with harsh passion. "We do not recognize that agreement as binding on all Hoomen for all time to come." He swung around so that he was speaking as much to the spectators as to the judge. "We see no reason why the Vramen should hold such restrictive power merely to bar us from attaining the long life they enjoy."

Hammond heard a low mutter of assent from the crowded rows of seats. Evidently most of the Hoomen in the hall felt the same resentment as Wilson. The sound from them was like the first low growl of a great angry animal. Yet Thayn and the three Vramen men sat with faces perfectly calm.

"The validity of our agreement with the Vramen is not in question here," said the judge. "It was made freely, as a small return for all the benefits the Vramen have conferred upon humanity. By breaking it, by using violence and fomenting hostility toward the Vramen, you have committed a crime of state. Since you can offer no extenuating circumstances, and since you have not protested the probe records, your guilt is beyond dispute. You are sentenced to life on the penal planet of Spica."

With quiet dignity Jon Wilson said, "We expected no other judgment. But a day will come when the Vramen domination of our whole civilization will be thrown off. And then we will take the secret of life from them."

Again a mutter of angry assent swept the spectators. It was silenced by the judge.

"Our sentence applies to all the defendants except the one named Kirk Hammond," he said. "I understand that the Vramen representatives here wish to ask for commutation of his sentence."

He looked at Thayn Marden. The Vramen woman rose and glanced at Hammond's defiant face as she spoke.

"That was our intention," she said, "but the man Kirk Hammond has utterly refused his cooperation, so we withdraw the request."

The judge looked down at Hammond, frowning. "That is unfortunate. Your history is known, and as a man cast by almost miraculous chance from your far past age into our time you would ordinarily be an admired and honored guest among us. But you have, by the evidence of the encephaloprobe, conspired with these others in full knowledge that you were breaking our laws. The exceptional circumstances of your personal history cannot justify overlooking your deliberate infraction of the law of the Federated Suns. Only if the Vramen representatives request it can I suspend your sentence."

"We are still quite willing to make the request if the man Hammond will agree to aid our historical researches," Thayn said calmly.

The judge said earnestly to Hammond, "I would advise you to comply with that request."

Hammond looked across at Thayn. He felt full of rage, against her for putting him into this position, against the Vramen for arrogating to themselves the space he had helped to conquer, against the whole universe for trapping him in this intolerable exile from his own world and time. And all of his frustrated rage and resentment came out in his answer.

"I'm damned if I will!"

"Then you must serve your sentence on Kuum, the penal planet of Spica," said the judge. "You will not be released unless you change your mind and agree to do as the Vramen ask."

Hammond walked out of the courtroom with the others, in a curious state of shock. It had all happened so fast and so smoothly that he had trouble realizing that he had actually been sentenced to a life term in prison.

"Isn't there any appeal?" he asked, of no one in particular. "Isn't there any parole, time off for good behavior—"

Wilson's voice answered him, cold and distant. "Every ten years they run a new series of 'probe tests. If the tests show that the prisoner has been completely rehabilitated—in other words, that he will not repeat his crime—he may be returned to society. But this needn't worry you, Hammond."

"Why not?"

"You heard Marden, so did we. The gates will open any time for you."

There was a pause, while their massed footsteps rang hollow in the high corridor, marching them toward the beginning of punishment.

Then Jon Wilson said softly, "Was that part of her promise to you, Hammond—part of the traitor's pay?"

Chapter 9

LONG AGO a boy in Ohio had cried, "*I want to out into space someday.*" And he had gone, toward the strangest doom in history.

And now Hammond was out in space again. But this time he was not in a little satellite but in a great star-ship, outward bound toward the vast deeps of interstellar space.

"Too big," he thought, feeling a numbness as he looked out through the port. "Too big, too far."

He was still a little dazed by it all. From the courtroom he and his fellow prisoners had been taken within a few hours by guarded cars, through the city Rurooma. His glimpses of the mighty pylons they passed between, towering stark and clean and shining from green parks, had been overpowering enough. But it was at the starport that the full impact of ten thousand years of change crushed him. He had thought of the base at Canaveral and the pitifully small and hopeful rocket, the little satellite it would try to push into an orbit around the Moon and back. And how small the memory of that seemed when he stood on a tarmac that ran for miles to the horizon and saw the vast and ordered confusion of cranes and shops and warehouses and launching pits.

And the ships.

Far removed indeed were these great ships of the starways from the unsteady little rockets of the Twentieth Century. Their dark hulls loomed vast as thunderclouds over the tiny men and vehicles that came and went around them. They rested now, but it was the rest of giants who had been to the far shores of infinity, who knew the ways of distant suns and worlds, whose sides were scarred by the drift of remote nebulae, and who would presently spurn this little planet

Earth from beneath them and return into the cosmic glare and gloom that was their home. And as they were taken toward one ship that had the Federated Suns insigne on its side, Hammond had seen the throngs that swirled through the starport, Hoomen from every part of the galaxy, red-skinned, green-skinned, pink and blue and gray-skinned, their pigmentation and appearance changed by generations of life under alien suns, but all of them fruit of Earth's far-flung seed.

Utterly different had been the take-off in the ship from the roaring climb on an oldtime rocket. He knew something of these star-ships, from his eager questions in the caverns. They were driven by a far-reaching development of the ion-drive suggested in his own time. Cesium was vaporized and its ions accelerated by the voltage of great generators to provide backward thrust through plasma-jets. Then a higher-speed photon drive took over, pushing the ship rapidly to many multiples of the speed of light, throwing it into "overdrive" by shifting it just a little out of ordinary three-dimensional space to escape the limiting mass-speed ratio.

Hammond and the others sat in recoil-chairs in the main cabin of the sealed prison-deck of the ship, and then the loud droning of generators was followed by a sudden sense of weight, growing and growing but so smoothly that at no moment was it unbearable. It had not even seemed to interest the others near him. Jon Wilson sunk in brooding silence, Quobba arguing with Tammas, all of them star-ship men or men well used to star-ships. They had not even bothered to look out. But Hammond did.

He was still looking out.

He knew this port was not really a window. You didn't really look through it, you looked into it, as into an oldtime television. It was a scanner with a mechanism more complex than any television inside it, one that translated twisted-up light-rays no one could see by into a picture that made sense, so that he seemed to look right out into space.

Hammond had seen space before, the hosts of stars marching forever across the black meadows of heaven, burning companies of hot gold and smoky red and ice-blue and green, trailing bannerets of nebulosity, a maze of light so vast that it was hard to think of each gleaming point as a mighty sun boiling with atomic fire as it plunged falling with its planets through infinity. He had seen this before but he watched it again with fascination as the sun Sol and its planets fell behind. He could not turn from the spectacle.

He looked and looked, and of a sudden it seemed that the ship had vanished from around him. He was alone in space and there was nothing but himself and the stars. They watched him with bright and pitiless eyes, and he looked back at them and could not see them, for he sat in the little satellite, frozen and blind and deathlike, through all the milennia following his lone unending orbit.

"—*count myself king of infinite space, were it not that I have bad dreams.*" It had been only a dream of the dead-alive Hammond that he was awakened to live again. He would never awaken, he would go on forever and ever. . . .

"Kirk!"

A voice pleading in his ear, a hand tugging at his arm, and abruptly the spell snapped and he was in the ship again, sick and shaking, with Iva Wilson pulling him away from the scanner.

"Your face," she whispered. "I couldn't stand it. It was—awful."

He had to make an effort to speak. "My old nightmare got me again. Self-hypnosis, I guess. Thanks, Iva."

The voice of Jon Wilson spoke up harshly behind them. "Let him be, Iva."

Hammond turned, a cold sweat still on him. Wilson and Gurth Lund had come up, and there were others behind them, and there was hostility on every face except the faces of Quobba and Tammas.

"Wait a minute," said Hammond. He was still shaking inside but he forced himself to speak. "I don't blame you for being angry. I was made a fool of, and I did a foolish thing. But I didn't betray you deliberately."

Jon Wilson's gaunt face did not soften. He said bitterly, "I could forgive a mistake, even though it's wrecked everything we worked for. But I don't think it was a mistake. I think you did deliberately make that signal at Marden's request."

"Father, you can't really think that!" Iva protested.

Anger was beginning to conquer Hammond's shakiness. He said, "Damn it, if I'd done that why would I refuse to help the Vramen when it meant my freedom?"

"That," said Wilson, "is what I would like to know. Unless the Vramen sent you along with us as a spy."

"You don't have a scrap of proof for such a charge," Hammond said hotly. "You—"

Wilson said, "Yes I have. As leader of the accused, it was my duty to examine the encephaloprobe records made before our trial."

Quobba and Lund and the others looked puzzled. But Hammond, with a sudden sinking sensation, guessed what was coming.

"I found in the 'probe record of your mind, Hammond, a clear indication that you love Thayn Marden."

A roar of anger burst from the others, and out of it Lund's voice rose clear and deadly, saying, "He betrayed us for her."

He charged at Hammond.

Surprised by the sudden fierce attack, Hammond was caught off guard. Lund's fist took him hard on the jaw, half stunned him, knocked him down, and then both Lund's hands were around his throat shutting off his breath, and Lund's face was above his in the darkening air as implacable and intent as a tiger's. With a savage effort, Hammond doubled his knees and sent Lund reeling back off him.

Wilson grabbed Lund and held him.

"No! You'll only bring the guards down here and get us all locked in our cabins."

Hammond got to his feet. He ignored Lund and the others. He spoke straight to Wilson.

"I did not betray you, not with intent. And I do not love Thayn Marden, no matter what the 'probe said."

Wilson said flatly, "A man can lie, a man can be mistaken, but the 'probe does not lie and it is never mistaken. Whether you sent that signal deliberately or not, a man who loves a Vramen can not be trusted."

He turned away, taking Iva with him, and the others followed him. Hammond looked after them in anger and frustration. The hell with them, he thought. If that was what they thought of him he might just as well accept the Vramen offer.

But when he thought of Thayn Marden he knew he would never do that. He wouldn't give that icy, unhuman imitation of a female that much satisfaction. He might resent the Hoomen's suspicions, but the Vramen he actively hated. It might be just because he felt uneasily inferior to them, but whether that was so or not he still detested their domination of space and their monopoly of the secret of life.

It came home to Hammond again that he was and always would be out of place in this age. He would never completely understand the psychology of these people, the abyss between his origin and theirs was too great. But he refused to give way to that feeling. If he did, disorientation and loneliness would push him over the brink into madness. He had to pick up his life and live it in this strange new universe, the best way he could.

"And I've made a fine start of it," he thought heavily. "With the only friends I had here all hating and distrusting me."

A bell rang softly and an annunciator spoke, informing the prisoners that it was meal-time. They trooped away forward, ignoring Hammond. He was not hungry and he remained where he was, not moving, until he heard a step behind him.

He turned sharply. It was Iva Wilson, and her dark, pretty face was unhappy as she looked at him.

"Kirk, I came back—I'm sorry about what happened."

"Then you don't believe I was a deliberate traitor?"

"Of course not," she said quickly. "It was Thayn Marden's doing." She paused, then asked, "Is it true that you're in love with her?"

"Hell, no!" he exploded. "She's beautiful and I was attracted to her. What man wouldn't be? And that got into my brain-record and they thought it meant I loved her. That's the truth."

Iva looked relieved. "I was sure it must be so. For a Hooman really to love a Vramen is too impossible."

"Your father said the Vramen never really marry or have children," Hammond said. "Is that what you mean—that they have no real emotions?"

"We don't really know what the Vramen are like emotionally," Iva said. "They're strange, unhuman." She went on earnestly, "Kirk, the others will realize in time that you're no traitor. We'll be on Kuum a long time, and Father and the rest will have time to think. Don't argue with them now and they'll come around."

"I hope so," Hammond said dubiously. "But I can't figure Gurth Lund ever warming up to me. Why does he hate me so?"

"It's the Vramen he hates, very bitterly," Iva said. "The girl he loved died of illness a few years ago. Ever since, he's had it on his mind that if the Hoomen had the secret of life she would not have died. My father is the same way. It was my mother's death that made him so fiercely determined to get the Vramen secret of life for the Hoomen."

She pointed out toward a region of the starry heavens thick-sown with stars, a glittering wilderness of close-clustered suns and nebulosity.

"How would you feel if you saw the person you most loved dying, and knew there was a secret out there that would have prevented it?"

Hammond stared at the far, shining magnificence of that star-crowded region. "The Trifid is out there, then?"

Iva nodded. "The Trifid—and Althar."

Hammond felt that he could perfectly understand Lund's bitterness and Wilson's fanatic determination. No wonder they hated the Vramen. He took Iva's hand.

"Thanks for believing in me. And no matter what the others think, I'm still with you, all the way."

Iva shook her head. "The fight's over, for us." She turned away. "I'd better go before anyone sees me here. Father would be very angry."

Her hand was still in Hammond's. On sudden impulse he bent and kissed her.

The touch of her mouth was warm and eager and dear. And yet—what devil put the thought into his head?—it was not the electric thrill that he had found in Thayn Marden's cool lips.

When she was gone, he looked for a long time at the stupefying distant wilderness of stars and shining gas. Great bastions and ramparts of suns gleamed hotly, like walls of eternal fire guarding—what? What was it the Vramen had in there that gave them almost endless life? Althar was a name that told nothing. What did that name mask? Of a sudden, forgetting his own situation, Hammond felt with overwhelming force the mystery and wonder of the galaxy, all the magic and marvels and enigmas that could exist inside this vast pinwheel of stars that rolled forever through the infinite.

He kept his resolve and determinedly overlooked the hostility of his fellow prisoners during the next "days". Sooner or later, when their first resentment had abated, he would be able to convince them he was no traitor. But he had to admit that in the meantime his ostracism was hard to bear in these close quarters.

The "days" went by, and inside the ship they were marked only by the sleep-period bells, and the regular inspection carried out by the captain of Federated Suns Police in charge. But if there was no change inside the ship, it was not so outside. Day by day the whole aspect of the constellations changed, and this was proof of the incredible speed at which the photon drive now hurled them across the galaxy. It was hard for Hammond to realize that hosts of other ships were out there, speeding through those vast starry spaces to red Antares or green Sirius or dim Algol. He could not as yet wholly grasp the magnitude of the galactic civilization that had been built in ten thousand years.

Twice Hammond awoke screaming and sweating in his cabin in the middle of the sleep-period, breaking frantically from that recurrent nightmare of being back in the satellite in frozen sleep. He did not think he would ever get over that, at least not as long as he was in space. The horror of it made him dread sleep when each "day" ended.

There came a time when the ship veered and disclosed the blazing white globe of Spica dead ahead. The unearthly velocities of the drive had taken them across scores of parsecs and they were approaching their destination.

The droning generators changed in key, dropping down the scale, as the ship curved in through the dazzling glare of Spica. By a cosmic freak of chance the great white sun had only one planet, Kuum. It was obvious that the unusual isolation of this world was the reason why it had been chosen as a penal planet.

Kuum was a black-and-white planet, to their eyes. It was no larger than Earth and it had small milk-white oceans and continents covered with blue-black jungle and occasional clearings of pale gray grass. As the ship swung in in its landing pattern they saw that there was one large cleared region scores of miles across, surrounded by the dark jungle. This space held cultivated fields and a small town of metal houses. Off some distance from the town was a spaceport, but the whole spaceport area was enclosed by a high barrier of pale, shimmering light.

"So this is Kuum," said Rab Quobba. "It's one of the few worlds I never visited or wanted to visit."

"They've got a damned tight set-up here," muttered Shau

Tammas. "Look at that force-wall around the spaceport."

Jon Wilson's voice sounded unutterably weary and dis-couraged as he said, "I see it. And I understand why no prisoner has ever escaped from this planet."

Chapter 10

SITTING IN a blaze of diamond sunlight, Hammond reached down and pulled a tuft of grass from beneath his feet. It was thick-bladed grass, and each blade was a curious mottled white-and-black that looked gray from even a little distance. The bit of soil adhering to the root was jet-black.

"Not Earth," thought Hammond. He told himself that again. "I am not on Earth, I am on a different world."

Try to realize the differentness. Breathe it in, in the warm and humid air with the curious pungent rankness in it that is not quite a perfume and not quite a stink. Feel it, in the odd lightness of your body that comes from a slightly dif-ferent gravitation. Look up and be dazzled by that different-ness, by the iridescent un-blue sky in which a too-big, too-bright, too-white sun sinks like a blazing emperor toward the horizon.

He looked slowly around. He sat on a bench in front of a long, low metal barrack. The building was one of a dozen such structures, and beyond the barracks the paved black street was bordered by neat, shining metal cottages with smooth gray grass and bright unfamiliar flowers around them. In the distance there was a thin black line where the fields around the small settlement gave way to dark, wild jungle.

It did not look like a penal colony to Hammond. It had startled him when he first saw it, with its neat houses, its women chattering from door to door and children playing in the streets. Men had been coming in from their day's work in the jungle in heavy power-trucks, a motley lot of Hoomen from every part of the galaxy, hailing their wives and children or staring curiously at the new arrivals, not looking like prisoners at all. It had taken Hammond a while to realize that conceptions of prisons had changed and that the Federated Suns civilization was too enlightened to use harsh punishments. Kuum was a detention world, not a place of punishment. There was not even a guard in sight.

Actually, it was the guards who were in a sense the prisoners here. Over in the direction he thought of as east, Hammond could glimpse the top of the highest spaceport tower. Between him and the tower was a curious constant shimmer in the air. That was the high barrier of almost invisible radiance that completely enclosed the spaceport, the guard offices and barracks, and the supply warehouses. When they had first come out of the ship after it landed, a Hooman guard officer showed them this surrounding barrier and explained that it was an electrodynamic field constantly generated from guard headquarters.

"If you touch it, it won't kill you," he said, "but you'll be unconscious for a very long time. Don't approach it, now or in the future."

He had made a signal toward the high cement tower, and a narrow section of the radiant barrier suddenly vanished. The prisoners went through it in single file, and then the barrier closed again.

"And it can only be turned off from the tower inside it," Quobba growled. "That's fine. That's just fine."

Then Hammond had understood. You could only escape from this world in a ship. And star-ships only landed in the spaceport area, where the electric barrier barred out all prisoners. So the prisoners were free of this whole world—but could not escape from it.

They had been assigned quarters in this town, family units to separate cottages and single men to barracks. They had hardly had time to look around before men returning from work in the jungle poured in and began asking eager questions. The babble of talk, the excited queries about far stars and galactic ports of which he had never heard, had been bewildering to Hammond. He had escaped from it to this bench outside, to stare and wonder and try to realize that he was far across the galaxy from Earth.

A man came out and sat beside him. Hammond turned quickly, on the defensive, but this man was a stranger to him. He had very intelligent eyes in a face that was of a curious gray pallor. It was the same complexion that North Abel had, but though this man's face was unwrinkled he looked in some indefinable way much older and more mature than Abel.

"I'm Thol Orr," he said. "You're Hammond of Earth?"

Hammond nodded. He asked, "Are you by any chance from Algol?"

"That's right. But I've been here on Kuum for quite a while." Orr went on, "They're saying in there that you're a spy for the Vramen."

Hammond's heart sank. After a moment he said heavily, "It's not true. But I can't convince them of it."

He was feeling hopeless about that. He had thought that sooner or later the resentment of the others would abate and they would listen to reason, but that had not happened. No one, not even Quobba, would speak to him directly. No one even seemed to see him. He had been most thoroughly sent to Coventry during the whole voyage and now it was beginning here on Kuum.

Damn Thayn Marden. He blamed her, not the Hoomen. The trick she had played on him had put him in this position. He had a savage desire to pay her and the whole Vramen race back for it.

Thol Orr was looking at him with deep interest. "They are also saying that you come from the far past. I find that much harder to believe."

Hammond explained, not much caring whether the man

95

believed it or not. When he was finished Thol Orr shook his head.

"An incredible story, and yet it's scientifically quite possible. I want to hear more of it. I'll have you assigned to my work-crew."

He explained that all work on Kuum was under the direction of the prisoners themselves. The Federated Suns paid a fixed wage to the men for clearing away the jungle that surrounded the settlement. They had power-dozers, trucks and other machines, but nothing that could be converted into a weapon. No guards bothered them except that a guard-officer made a short inspection trip through the settlement each evening.

"You'll have a less rough time of it working in my crew, with all this hostility against you," the Algolian added.

"Then you don't believe I'm a Vramen spy?"

Thol Orr smiled. "The Vramen have no need of spies. That's only the old Hooman hatred of them talking."

"You don't seem to hate them so much," said Hammond curiously.

Thol Orr shrugged. "It was the Vramen who sent me here. But on the other hand, they could much more easily have killed me—and they didn't." He went on to elaborate. "I was a physicist of some note, once. My enthusiasm for research got the best of me. I was doing some in the field, in a small chartered ship, and strayed too near the Trifid."

Hammond looked at him with sudden intense interest. "You were hunting for Althar?"

"No, not at all. I was studying cosmic radiation and came across some odd spectra near the Trifid. I got too interested and went too close. The Vramen could legally have detonated our ship, but they didn't. I was given a life-sentence on Kuum, and my hired crew got five years. Quite lenient, I thought."

The sun had set and the dusk was passing into a moonless night. Unfamiliar constellations glittered hotly in the sky, and away beyond the lights of the little town the barrier around the spaceport shimmered out like a strange aurora. Thol Orr stood up and stretched.

"We rise early," he said, "so you had better get as much sleep as you can."

Hammond followed him unwillingly into the big communal main room of the barrack, hating to face what he knew awaited him. All the sixty or seventy occupants of the building were gathered around the newcomers at one end of the room. He heard Quobba's voice rumbling as he entered, and from the excited comments of the others he knew that Quobba had been telling them of Jon Wilson's frustrated plans.

"By all the suns, I wish you'd made it!" cried a fat, pink man. "If we could get Hooman hands on whatever's at Althar—"

"Cut it, for now," Gurth Lund said curtly.

He was looking at Hammond, and all eyes turned in the same direction. Hammond thought that he had never seen such a circle of hostile faces, staring at him. He wanted to speak to them, to try again to convince them that he was neither a traitor nor a spy, but he realized that they would not even listen to him. He turned and went into the little sleeping room that had been assigned to him.

Lying in the dark little room, Hammond felt his anger slowly crystallize into a savage determination. These Hoomen hated and suspected him because his folly had wrecked their dream of reaching Althar. All right, he would make them eat that hatred and suspicion. He would do so by getting them and himself out of this planetary prison so they could carry out that quest for Althar. He didn't know how he would do it but he would do it somehow, soon or late. He'd show them how much he loved the Vramen!

Next morning Hammond ate his breakfast in silence, no man speaking to him. But when the work-crews were announced, Thol Orr called his name.

"You can ride in the cab with me," Orr said, as they went out to the waiting trucks. Men were already climbing into them. Hammond did not look forward to riding with them, but he said,

"They'll all be down on you too if you talk to me."

Thol Orr smiled. "I don't think so. I've been here so long. But I'll risk it anyway. I want to talk about the past."

By the time they crossed the cleared land and reached the edge of the jungle, the glaring orb of Spica had already risen well into the sky. The warm, humid air brought a dank mist from the tenebrous glades of the forest. Hammond had never seen anything like this black jungle. It was a forest out of some demoniac painter's fevered imagination, a bewildering tangle of glossy black trees and shrubs whose ebony limbs bore great masses of pale gray leaves. There were looping black vines, and enormous pure-white flowers, and strange featherless and songless birds flitting among the gray fronds.

The trees and brush had to be rooted out with the power-dozers. As fast as a small section was cleared it was plowed deeply and chemicals were mixed into the soil to inhibit the growth of the rank jungle plants and allow the gray grass to spring up instead.

"You'll handle one of the chains," Thol Orr told Hammond. "We pull the larger trees out by main force."

Hammond found himself working with the others of the motley little crew under the Algolian's orders.

"Fasten your chain around that tree—no, lower down," Thol Orr called. "Now stand clear."

The power-dozer, driven by a heavy atomic motor, sank its spiked tracks into the ground and yanked the tree forth. Flights of huge insects, like giant dragon-flies, skittered from its branches as it fell. The sun poured down ever more hotly. Crawler-vines writhed down from trees and looped around Hammond's body, tiny sucker-roots trying to fasten onto his arms and face. He tore the uncanny plants loose. By late afternoon Hammond was hot and tired but felt he had got the routine of the work. But he quickly found that he still had much to learn about the jungles of Kuum.

He was pulling one of the drag-chains into the thick brush ahead of the crew when he smelled a peculiarly heavy, musky odor. Next moment he bumped into a round black mound higher than his head. The black mound came suddenly alive. It heaved slightly and from beneath it a huge horny paw reached out and grasped Hammond.

Crushed, half stunned, he felt himself being dragged back toward the mound he now recognized as a giant shelled turtle-like creature. Hammond was near the beast's body when the paw that dragged him stopped. It held onto him, but a sharp tremor ran through it and through the whole huge body.

Half conscious, unable even to cry for help in the crushing grip of that enormous paw, Hammond felt lost. The others were out of sight beyond the thick brush. His brain whirled and darkened, and all he could think of was that it was crazy and impossible for him to have survived all that he had to die in this brute's grasp on this distant world.

Other and more violent tremors ran through the huge body. The great paw weakened and relaxed. Then Hammond saw something that made him doubt his sanity. The whole horny carapace was splitting wide open. As he crawled away from the creature he saw the ghastly final phase of the incredible change. From out of the split remains of the body there climbed a much smaller creature of exactly the same species.

"Thol Orr!" yelled Hammond, getting to his feet and stumbling away.

The Algolian answered his cry by driving his power-dozer right through the brush. The smaller black creature that had emerged from the broken body of the larger one scuttled hastily away into the jungle.

"A mud-phoenix," said Thol Orr. "Did it harm you?"

Hammond told him what had happened, and the Algolian whistled.

"You were lucky. You blundered into the thing just at the time of its rebirth, and that's all that saved you." He went on to explain. "The mud-phoenix is asexual and reproduces itself by that messy cycle of sudden death and rebirth. They're dangerous when they're full grown. Didn't the other men warn you that a musky odor means there's one around?"

"No. They didn't warn me," said Hammond shortly.

He knew now how much they hated him. They had deliberately let him walk into the thing.

Their enmity was further emphasized when they all returned to the settlement that evening. The other men talked over the day's work, gathered in the small drinking-shops, hailed friends in the darkening streets. But when Hammond came by, no one spoke to him and he got only unfriendly stares. He saw Iva Wilson at the door of a cottage but she hung her head and turned away from him and went inside. He understood that Jon Wilson had forbidden any further talk with him.

Only Thol Orr talked with him, and lent him books and helped him to learn the written language. But Hammond suspected that he did so only because of his deep scientific interest in Hammond's survival from the distant past. The others did not have enough of that interest to counterbalance their hatred.

Let them hate him, Hammond thought. They had a right to. Wait till his chance came, a chance to pay back Thayn and all the Vramen. A traitor, was he, and a Vramen spy? He would ram that idea down their throats.

Holding to that grim determination, Hammond brooded over plans of escape as the days passed. No prisoner had ever got away from Kuum. The great reason was the fact that few star-ships ever came here, and when one did come it stayed inside the barrier of the spaceport area into which prisoners could not go.

He kept running up against that insurmountable obstacle of the force-wall, discarding this plan and that because of it, and then he suddenly realized that he alone of all the prisoners here did have a way to get to a star-ship. Suddenly everything was clear. He thought out every detail in his long lonely hours, and he had plenty of them, until he was sure just how everything would go.

Then he realized that there was still another obstacle.

"It won't work unless the others follow me," he thought. "But they won't. They won't even listen to me. They'd think I was leading them into a Vramen trap."

And there it stood.

Weeks of labor in the jungle made Hammond hardy and sun-blackened and grimly accustomed to constant loneliness. He had learned to drive the power-dozers and was taking one of them along the edge of the jungle to where Thol Orr and his crew waited for the replacement vehicle, when he heard a choking cry from inside the brush.

The yell was cut off. But there had been in it a quality of desperate appeal that made Hammond swing his machine around and send it crashing into the brush.

A cold musky taint hit his nostrils and then he saw ahead the big shelled black mound of a mud-phoenix, one almost as large as the one he had escaped on his first day. The grotesque paws were just drawing a man in. Hammond rammed the heavy dozer right at the thing, aiming to miss the man but knock the brute away from him. The impact of collision hurled him out of his seat and he crashed into the brush. He got up to find that the dozer had run right over the mud-phoenix before its safety-control stopped it.

A few feet away the man who had been caught by the phoenix was scrambling to his feet, and Hammond saw that it was Rab Quobba, fouled with mud and slime but unhurt enough to stand staring at him with an expression of peculiar embarrassment.

"Hammond," he said. And then, "Thanks. I—" He stopped, swore, and came forward to grasp Hammond's hand. "I've been a damned fool."

"I see," said Hammond harshly. "Because I happen to save your neck, all of a sudden I'm not a Vramen spy any longer."

Quobba shuffled his feet and said ruefully, "I never did

believe that, to tell you the truth. I was just boiling mad because you let that Vramen wench wreck all our plans."

Hammond stopped bristling. "Well, you had a right to be," he said. And then suddenly he realized that here was the opportunity he had been waiting for. He grabbed it. "Quobba, listen. Would you and the others escape from here and try for Althar again, if you could?"

Quobba said, "We would." His eyes narrowed, became bright and sharp. "How could we?"

"It'll take Wilson and all his people to help. They can run a star-ship, if we get our hands on one. But they won't trust me. They'd follow you."

"What's your idea?"

Hammond said, "There'll be a star-ship coming here soon—"

Quobba interrupted. "No. Not for almost a month. The last supply-ship was just here."

Hammond smiled. "I can *make* a ship come any time I choose, and not a supply-ship, either."

"Well," said Quobba, "go on. I'll listen."

He listened, and Hammond talked, and the Vegan's face got longer and longer, and when Hammond stopped he shook his head.

"It won't be easy. And you'd be taking the biggest share of the risk." He was silent a minute and then he said, "But it might work."

"Will you go along with it?"

Quobba grinned. "I'm a star-man. I never did take to grubbing in the dirt. What do I do?"

"I'll start things moving right away," Hammond said. "You talk to the others, get them ready to follow you in a break. Just don't mention my name, that's all. Tell them you have a plan in mind but you don't want to tell it yet."

Quobba nodded. "I'll get them on their toes. But Hammond—you better look out. What you're going to do to-night will make the others more bitter against you than ever."

"I know that," said Hammond, and went away.

When the guard officer came through the barrack that evening on his usual inspection tour, Hammond stepped out and spoke to him.

"I have a request to make," he said, and saw that instantly the other prisoners turned to watch and listen.

"What is it, Hammond?"

"When I was sentenced to my term here," Hammond said carefully, "the court told me that whenever I was willing to cooperate with the Vramen in their historical researches, my sentence would be suspended. I am now willing to do so. Will you notify your authorities and also Thayn Marden, the chief Vramen representative at Earth?"

The officer was a loyal servant of the Federated Suns but he was a Hooman and not without Hooman prejudices. He stiffened a little and looked at Hammond with unfriendly eyes.

"Very well. I'll have a message sent to Earth at once."

When he had gone, Gurth Lund and the others glared at Hammond. "So you're going to quit spying and go back to your Vramen friends, are you?" Lund said.

Hammond did not answer. There was so much raw hatred of him in the room now that he felt a single word would bring an explosion.

The guard officer came back three hours later.

"Your request has been granted by the Federated Suns officials at Earth. Thayn Marden, representing the Vramen, will come at once to Kuum. She will interrogate you, and if she is satisfied of your sincerity you will be paroled."

"Thank you," said Hammond.

The officer left.

There was a strained silence. Hammond started toward his room. He looked at the faces of his fellow-prisoners as he went, and he thought that he would have to take care every moment now. He thought that he would be lucky if he was still living when that star-ship came.

Chapter 11

A SOUND vast as the voice of God filled the sunlit heavens, a thunderous roar that hammered the dark jungle into silence and made great echoes that bawled and bantered overhead. The men, in the act of climbing into the trucks, stopped and stared upward, squinting against the white blaze of the sinking sun.

Hammond, looking with sudden tenseness, saw the low scattered clouds boil and swirl. Then the fleecy vapors rolled and parted and down through them came a long black shape, dropping toward the spaceport fast, fast.

Thol Orr looked down at him from the cab of the truck. "That will be it?"

"I think so," said Hammond. A breathless excitement was taking hold of him. "I hope so."

"We'll soon know," said the Algolian, and started the motor.

As the truck rolled and lumbered out of the edge of the jungle and across the cleared fields, Hammond felt tension growing in him. He had been waiting many days for the ship, for the moment. And they had not been easy days. Only Quobba knew the truth, everyone else regarded him as a proved traitor. He felt that Lund, and a good many others, would kill him if he had a chance. Hammond had been careful in the jungle not to give anyone that chance. Even Iva Wilson had looked at him with stony contempt when he encountered her.

There had been only one exception to the general feeling and that was Thol Orr. The Algolian had only said,

"So you're going to cooperate with the Vramen? Perhaps it's for the best."

"You don't seem to hate the Vramen as much as most people do," Hammond had said. "Even though they sent you here."

Thol Orr shrugged. "Well, I'm a scientist. And the Vramen are the greatest of scientists. The inventions they've given as in past centuries are what have enabled Hoomen to spread all over the galaxy."

"But don't you resent it that they hoard the secret of unlimited life for themselves?"

"I don't know," said the Algolian. "I suppose I do resent it unconsciously. I'm sure that if I were dying I'd hate them frantically. On the other hand, the Vramen lead such dedicated, hard, barren lives that I don't envy them their immortality."

But Thol Orr was alone in his tolerant viewpoint. The others hated the Vramen and hated Hammond as a creature of the Vramen. The only exceptions there were Quobba and Tammas, who knew the truth. The little Mizarian, always the shadow of his big Vegan friend, had been let into Hammond's secret and twice Hammond had found opportunities to confer secretly with them. He had asked many questions of them, particularly about the non-lethal shocker weapons and about the probable control-mechanism of the electro-dynamic barrier. And Quobba had told him that he had prepared some of the boldest spirits for a break, without mentioning Hammond at all.

Now the slowly growing tension of the long waiting days was approaching its climax, and Hammond found himself jumpy as a cat as they drove back to the settlement. A guard was waiting in the barrack when he entered. He spoke to Hammond without love.

"A ship has arrived from Earth. Thayn Marden of the Vramen is here to interrogate you. Come along."

Hammond's pulse quickened. The others watched him with bitter hatred as he started after the guard. He looked back meaningly at Rab Quobba and the Vegan played up to the cue. He strode into the corridor after Hammond, swearing furiously.

"It's blasted good riddance of you!" he bellowed. "I hope I never see your damned traitor's face again!"

Once out in the corridor, Quobba dropped his voice to a whisper and asked hastily,

"Now? Tonight?"

Hammond nodded quickly. "Get Wilson and the others to walk near the barrier. I'll do my best."

The guard looked back and Quobba began again to roar curses after Hammond as he walked away.

There was a small ground-car with another guard at the wheel. They entered, and the car sped out of the neat little town toward the distant spaceport. Spica was a great white flame on the horizon, glancing in glittering shafts off the shining metal roofs. People in the street looked at the passing car. From the door of her father's cottage Iva Wilson looked too, and then turned her back and went inside. He knew she had seen him. It occurred to him that if he failed in his attempt, she might never know that he hadn't really gone over to the Vramen.

Of a sudden, the weariness and tension of these weeks of hatred triggered a reaction in Hammond. He thought: And why not go over to the Vramen? Why not, and to the devil with all these people who were so ready to call him a spy and worse?

No. He couldn't. The Hoomen were not his people, though they came closer to it than the Vramen. But this wasn't a matter of loyalty to a particular group. To Hammond, it was loyalty to an ideal from ten thousand years ago. He had risked death and he had died, almost, to win the freedom of the stars for men. Not if he could help it was anyone going to abridge or limit that freedom. Not the Vramen, nor anyone else. He was going through on that all the way.

He thought that it might be ridiculous of him to pit himself against the near-immortals who dominated the life of the galaxy. They had knowledge, vast knowledge, of things he'd never even heard about. But he might, he just might, carry this through in spite of that.

He would do it or die trying, if for no other reason than the childish but very powerful desire to see Wilson and Lund and all the rest of them including Iva eat crow.

The car approached the shimmering barrier and stopped. The guard leaned out and made a signal toward the high tower inside. Again, as on the day when Hammond had arrived here, a narrow section of the barrier vanished. The car rolled quickly through that opening, and the web of force instantly sprang shut again behind them.

Hammond's pulses hammered as they sped toward the complex of buildings. Beyond the buildings, out on the wide tarmac of the spaceport, towered a black star-ship of comparatively small size. Its base was in shadow but its tip was high enough to catch the last rays of the setting sun, and it was like a great dark hand grabbing for the dying light.

It was a hand that could grab for Althar and the greatest secret of infinity, he thought.

The main building was ahead, a three-level oblong white block with a square tower at one end rising several levels higher. The top of the tower was a room with all its walls transparent, glowing in the dusk. Hammond looked up at it casually as he went with the two Hoomen into the building. That would be the spaceport control-room. The commandant's headquarters were in the tower under it, if the information Quobba had gathered from older prisoners was correct.

It was correct. Hammond was taken through corridors to a lift that jumped smoothly upward. He came out into another hallway above. He glanced covertly at two stairways that led up. One of them must be a way to the control-room.

The commandant of the guards of Kuum was a tall man with the faintly greenish skin of a Hooman from Sirius. But Hammond hardly glanced at him when he first entered the office. He had eyes only for Thayn Marden.

Thayn turned from the window beside which she had been standing, and her blue eyes searched his face quickly. He had forgotten, he thought, how beautiful she was. In the black shorts and shirt that made her white limbs and ashen blonde hair stand out, with the jewelled badge of the Vramen glittering on her breast, she was breathtaking.

She said, "You're willing now to cooperate with our historians, to gain your freedom?"

Hammond nodded. "I might as well. The Hoomen think I'm a traitor to them anyway." It was easy to sound bitter.

"If you'll answer some preliminary questions to prove your sincerity," Thayn said, "I'll take you back to Earth. You'll work there with a special group of Vramen historians."

Hammond looked at the commandant. "I've a certain condition to make first. But—it's for your ears alone, Marden."

The commandant shook his head. "The rules do not permit—"

Thayn said, "There'll be no danger. Give me your shocker and wait outside."

The commandant still looked doubtful, but he bowed and said, "Very well, if you wish it."

He took a little black plastic tube from the case at his belt that contained it and handed it to Thayn. He went out of the room and closed the door.

Thayn held the shocker in front of her and said quietly, "Keep at that distance. Now what is this condition that's so confidential?"

Hammond nerved himself for the part he had to play. So far, so good. But everything now depended on the next few minutes.

"Thayn, it isn't just freedom I'm doing this for," he said. "It's you. I want to see you, be near you again."

She looked at him, coolly, cynically. "Why?"

"Because I'm in love with you," Hammond said. "I'm the prize fool of the universe, but I can't help it."

He expected her to laugh, to get angry, to voice some expression of contempt or call him a liar. She did none of these things. He thought he must have put some real conviction in his voice, because she stared at him and there was suddenly a strange, strained look in her white face.

"No," she said finally. "It's not possible. Don't ever talk of love between you and me."

"Why not?" he demanded. "You may be immortal or nearly so, but you're still a woman. And I love you."

"You don't know what you're saying. No Vramen can love or marry in the way you mean—especially a Hooman. You haven't the faintest idea of all that stands between us."

Hammond was elated. She had not doubted him at all. He had gambled on that, gambled on her acceptance of the encephaloprobe record that had mistaken physical desire for love. He was lying in his teeth when he talked of loving her, but the lie was only a just return for what she had done to him. He hoped it worked as well.

He took a step toward her and spread out his hands in a gesture of appeal, speaking with all the passion he could pretend.

"Thayn, it doesn't make sense! Why couldn't a Vramen marry a Hooman?"

There was a look of pain in her face, and her voice was so low he could hardly hear it.

"I can't tell you why. But you can believe me when I say that it would be easier for you to cross the ages back to your own time than to cross what separates us."

She had never looked more beautiful than she did at this moment, standing before him with that strange look of doubt and pain. Hammond found it easy, very easy, to counterfeit passion. He took a step closer.

"Thayn, listen to me. Whatever separates us, we could overcome it—"

She was shaking her head, her blue eyes haunted with a secret misery, as he took that step closer.

He swung his fist and hit her hard on the chin.

Thayn fell without a sound. He grabbed her and caught

her before she hit the floor, but the plastic shocker dropped from her limp hand and rolled across the floor. He eased her down and hastily retrieved the weapon. Then he stood for a moment, breathing hard and trembling, looking down at Thayn's still white face.

His trick had worked. It had put Thayn off guard for the crucial moment he needed. But somehow he had not expected her to react to his avowal of love in quite the way she had. It almost seemed as though she—

He told himself that he was a fool to stand here wasting precious seconds. He examined the shocker, driven now by a feverish haste. These non-lethal weapons were the only ones permitted by the laws of the Federated Suns, such instruments of destruction as Jon Wilson's vortice-gun being utterly taboo. From what Quobba had told him, the shocker was merely a capacitor which held a certain electrical charge. The slide on the tube released a portion of the charge in a wave of electromagnetic energy tuned exactly to overload the electroencephalic circuits of the human brain, producing unconsciousness. The drawbacks of the thing as a weapon were its extremely short range and the fact that in use the charge was rapidly exhausted.

Hammond gripped the thing in his hand and went to the door that led to the outer office. He opened it with a sudden movement.

There were three men in the room—an orderly, the commandant, and the guard who had brought him here. They turned and when they saw Hammond there alone with the shocker in his hand they moved fast.

Not fast enough. Hammond pressed the slide on the tube forward. There was no visible emanation from it, but it buzzed like an angry rattlesnake. He swept it back and forth with frantic awkwardness. The three charging men staggered and fell crashing to the floor.

It was so quick that it took Hammond a moment to realize he had dropped them and that he was wasting the shocker's limited charge. He hastily slid back the control.

Now what?

The stairs. One of them must lead to the control-room above.

He stuck his head cautiously out into the corridor. He heard distant voices from other offices, but no one was in the corridor. He ran across it to the nearest of the two stairs, and started up it.

His heart was pounding but he felt a certain heady zest.

He had never done anything like this before, he had been a scientific student and not a soldier or man of action, and there was a delightful wickedness in all this that was a little intoxicating.

There was a closed door at the top of the stair. It might lead into the control-room or into a hornet's nest of guards. In his excited mood, Hammond didn't much care which. He pulled the door open.

It was the control-room. The transparent walls looked out on four sides across the now dark spaceport, toward the glowing shimmer of the electrodynamic barrier. In the center of the room was a U-shaped bank of control panels, with gauges, switches, scanners, and many little blinking lights. There was a guard inside this U peering into something that looked like a radar screen. There was another guard at the right-hand wall, looking out. The backs of both were to Hammond.

He pointed the shocker at the back of the man looking out and pressed the slide. The tube buzzed and the man fell.

The man in the U of switchboards turned a stricken, staring face toward Hammond. Hammond turned the shocker on him.

The shocker did not buzz. He realized suddenly that his inexpert handling had exhausted its charge.

The man in the U grabbed a mike and screeched into it. "Tower calling! Escaped prisoner—"

Hammond ran in and banged him on the head with the black shocker-tube. He had never hit anyone on the head that way before and he expected the fellow to fall right down but he did not. Instead he howled with pain and fury and ducked down to shelter his head, still yelling his alarm into the mike. Hammond, desperate, grabbed him by the hair and banged his head hard against the switch-panel. This time the man fell, tearing out of his grasp.

Bells went off somewhere down in the main part of the building.

"Oh, damn it," said Hammond, groaning. He didn't feel any delightful excitement now. He had botched it, he was a miserable failure at this sort of thing.

Say less than a minute before someone got up here. Lock the door? No, there was no lock on it, no reason for one in a building where unauthorized persons were never allowed. How many seconds did he have to find the right controls? Not many. Not enough, probably.

He did a sort of frantic shuffle along the panels, peering at the legends underneath each back of controls. Most of them he could not understand. Iva and Thol Orr had taught him Hooman writing but not every technical term in the book. But he was not trying to read them all. He was searching for a particular legend that meant "Field Generator Control", which Quobba had taught him with great care. He couldn't possibly find it in all this complexity. . . .

He found it.

It was under a big rheostat with a bar as long as his arm and a knob at the end of the bar. Hammond grabbed it and swung it back around to the symbol that meant zero.

As he ran out from the U of panels toward the nearest window, he heard feet starting to pound up the stairs.

Hammond yelled when he looked out. It seemed six times as dark out there as before, for there was no shimmering, glowing barrier around the spaceport area now. And from two, three, no, four or five places around the compound the dark figures of men were running in. Rab Quobba had been as good as his word, the prisoners had been ready and they were swarming into the spaceport in scores. Bells chattered hysterically as guards startled by the first break in the history of the planet tumbled out of wherever they were. But at least a hundred prisoners were in now, and more coming. . . .

The door banged open behind Hammond and he started to spin around but there was a buzzing sound and the universe exploded into blackness.

Nothing.

For a timeless period, nothing at all. And then a voice saying, "He's coming around."

Coming around what? Not around the Moon, they sent you out but you can't go home again, you can only go around and around the track in space you've followed for a hundred centuries, around and around. . . .

"Hammond?"

He knew that voice. He tried to open his eyes and couldn't. After a moment he tried again, and could.

Thol Orr was looking down at him. Beyond the interested face of the Algolian he saw a curved metal ceiling, with a light glowing in it. He had seen a ceiling like that before. He had heard before the kind of heavy droning sound he could both hear and feel now.

He tried to whisper. "I thought I was in space—"

Thol Orr nodded. "You are." And then he said quickly, "Don't try to talk too much or get up yet. Your nerves are recovering from the shocker but it will take a little more time."

The shocker? Then Hammond remembered. He stared and now beyond Thol Orr he saw Iva Wilson looking down at him, anxious, joyous, smiling.

"We took the spaceport, Kirk," she said. "And we took the ship. They dropped the barrier again but it was too late, too many prisoners were in by then. We only learned from Quobba after the fight that it was you who raised the barrier."

"You took the ship?" he repeated. "Then this—"

"We're in it." Her eyes flashed. "We're on our way, we've been going for hours. On our way to the Trifid."

For a moment, weak as he still was, Hammond felt a sharp surge of elation. Then he remembered something and a chill crept over him.

"—thirty-four of us aboard," Iva was saying. "All of us who worked and planned in the caverns and a few others. And after what you did, we wouldn't leave *you* behind."

Hammond's strength was returning. He sat up, holding to the side of the bunk for support. He looked at Thol Orr and asked,

"You came too. Why?"

The Algolian shrugged. "They thought that with my past experience at the Trifid I could help sneak this ship in. Anyway, Kuum has become a little tedious. If we're recaptured they'll send me back there, but in the meantime what have I to lose?"

"You know damn well what you have to lose," Hammond said. "Your life. This ship isn't like the one Iva's people were building in the caverns. This has the Vramen detonator built into it like every ship, doesn't it?"

Thol Orr nodded. "It does."

"And if we're detected, they can press a key and blow us to fragments, can't they?"

Again Orr nodded. "They can. But Wilson and the others don't think they will."

"Why not?"

"We brought along a hostage," said Iva. "One of the Vramen. Thayn Marden."

Chapter 12

THERE HAD been a man named Goddard once, who watched his little rockets go up into the New Mexican sky and dreamed of the day when they would go farther. There had been a man named Oberth who planned the first conquest of space. A Laika dog had died, and a man named Kirk Hammond had as good as died, and many another man back in the Twentieth Century had given his thought and toil and life to the cause of setting man free in space.

And this was what all their sacrifices had been for, this ship in which Hammond now was. He had been in a ship like this before, but in a sealed prison-deck. Now he was in the pilot-room of a star-ship hurtling through infinity. He was glad that a freak of fate had let him live to see this. He wished that the other men he had worked with at Canaveral, all the men who had dreamed of this, could be here to see it.

"It gets you, doesn't it," said Quobba, without turning his head, from the pilot-chair.

"Yes," said Hammond a little unsteadily. "It does."

It was not only the vista through the forward viewplates that was overwhelming, this time. It was stunning enough, that view of the galactic wilderness. Colossal ramparts of scattered and clotted suns rose up in front of them, gleaming hotly in clusters like great hives of stars or shining out like foggy witchfires through the farflung nebulae. A dark cloud brooded to the left, with the starlight from behind it forming a shining halo around it. Close ahead to the right hung a magnificent double star whose components were pale yellow and smoky red, and the size of those two suns increased visibly as he watched.

But it was the ship itself that was most overwhelming to Hammond now. Especially this pilot-room, this small and crowded place where the minds of frail little human men forced a hurtling bulk of metal through the universe in the way they wanted it to go. In front and on either side of Quobba were three panels crowded with dials and ground-glass discs and graduated knobs. At intervals a figure or symbol would flash on one of the discs and Quobba would instantly adjust a knob to a new setting. The dim drone of the drive never changed or faltered.

Thol Orr had brought Hammond here and the Algolian

spoke now from behind him. "Technically, this control-room is vestigial. I mean, the star-ship could actually be flown by the big computer you saw in the calc-room. It does fly the ship when it goes on auto-pilot, for it uses ultra-radar and doesn't need vision. But psychologically, there's a need for men to feel that they themselves fly the ship and that's why we still use this set-up."

Quobba looked around with a grin on his battered blue face. "Luckily for me, all I have to do is handle the controls and let the computer figure the course. Want to try it?"

"Me?" said Hammond. "Why, no, I couldn't—I—"

"I'll be right behind you," said Quobba, getting out of the chair. "Go ahead. Lord knows you've earned the right."

Unbelievingly, Hammond slid into the chair. As the shining symbols and figures flashed, Quobba leaned over and showed him how to set the controls. He sat there and heard Quobba and Thol Orr talking behind him, about the course, about Althar. But their voices faded out of his hearing and there was nothing but the drone of the drive. There was nothing but stars and space and the ship, and himself.

"You've earned the right." Yes, he had earned it. Lots of others had too, back in the dawn of the space age. But destiny had decreed that he should be the one to live through to this time. And here was the dream made manifest and real, the aspiration of many men come at last to splendid fruition. His fingers touched the knobs in a caress. He sat and flew the ship and looked ahead into the stars.

He looked too long. For of a sudden, Hammond's high elation faded away in a strange self-hypnosis. He stared at the shining hosts and could not turn his gaze away. How could he turn, with his body frozen iron-hard? He had not moved for centuries, he would not move ever again, he would sit frozen in the little satellite and keep up his eternal and awful patrol in space. . . .

Hammond felt that dread nightmare memory overwhelming him again. He struggled against it, but in vain. And then, abruptly, he ceased to struggle. Stop trying to push it out of your mind, he told himself. Remember it, realize it, accept it. Yes, you were dead in nearly every sense of the word. Yes, your frozen form moved as a bit of cosmic debris among the drift for ten thousand years while the generations came and went. It was a terrible thing and also it was splendid. No man ever was or ever will be so long a part of space as you. Do not shudder at the memory of your pseudo-death. Be proud that destiny picked you to be one with the cosmic vastness of space and stars. Look the stars in the eyes as you did for ten thousand years, and know them for your brothers.

And slowly the hypnotic tension lifted from Hammond's mind and he did look into the bright hot eyes of the stars without dread. The nightmare quality was all gone from his memories, and he did not think that it would ever return again.

Behind him, Thol Orr said, "I have to leave you. We are to have a council of war and there are things I must get ready."

Hammond, staring and dreaming, hardly heard him and did not even turn. Rab Quobba smiled.

The council was many hours later in the big crew-room of the ship. Forty-odd men and women from many worlds gathered here, all who were not actually on duty in the ship. Jon Wilson sat with Lund and Quobba behind a table. Hammond, sitting with Iva among the others, still smarted from Wilson's greeting to him.

"Let us be clear, Hammond," said Wilson. "We owe you our escape, this last chance at Althar. We feel we can trust you in all things but one."

"And that one?"

"Marden," said Wilson grimly. "You're not to see her alone again. Oh, yes, we know how you handled her back at Kuum, but in view of that 'probe record we don't want you talking to her."

He added, holding out his hand, "In everything else, you're one of us again."

Hammond thought resentfully now that they might forget that damned 'probe record, after what he'd done. Then he became interested in Wilson's crisp explanation of their position.

"The mathematical probabilities of our successfully entering the Trifid are very low," he said. "On the other hand, we have a better chance than any Hooman has had for generations, so it seems we should make the attempt. Is that agreed?"

There was a murmur of assent. No excitement, no bravado, but a nodding of heads and a word from each.

"How long have we got?" asked Tammas, and Wilson turned to Lund. "You've been figuring that, Gurth."

Lund nodded and picked up a sheet of paper. "We smashed the telaudio transmitter at Kuum, and all spare parts, before we left. They can't send out an alarm and they have no ship. But their silence, the cessation of their daily report, will undoubtedly cause an investigation to be made within twenty-four hours."

He referred to the sheet. "The Federated Suns police base nearest to Kuum is at Alto Four. It will take ten days for a ship to go from there to Kuum."

"So that we have ten days before a general alarm goes out?" said Quobba. "That should be enough. We'll be to the Trifid before then."

Lund said sourly, "There's a variable in my equations. If a police cruiser happens to be in space nearer Kuum than Alto Four, it will undoubtedly be detailed to investigate. That would cut our ten days down considerably. Perhaps even to a day."

Their faces got longer at that information. But Hammond was thinking of something else. He asked,

"Suppose we get to the Trifid. I take it we'll be challenged by the Vramen from somewhere inside when they radar us?"

Thol Orr answered that. "That's what happened when they caught me. I suddenly got a telaudio challenge and an order to remain where I was and await arrest or our ship would be detonated."

"What do we do if we get such a challenge and order?" Hammond asked.

He was thinking of what Iva had said, that they were holding Thayn Marden as a hostage. He saw Iva glance swiftly at him.

Jon Wilson was frowning. "If we show them we have Marden aboard—"

"It won't stop them from detonating us," Thol Orr said quietly. "Believe me, the Vramen won't hesitate to sacrifice one of their own number to keep us from reaching Althar. My way is the only way."

"What way?" asked Quobba puzzledly.

"Thol Orr has prepared certain instruments that may help us," Wilson said evasively, and turned to Lund. "Bring Marden now."

Hammond felt his back go up. Were they going to start that encephaloprobe business again? He didn't like it one bit better than he ever had, and anyway he didn't see what good it would do.

Lund returned with Thayn Marden. There was still a bruise on her small chin. She looked intently at Hammond as she passed him, and her look surprised him. It was not the look of flaming resentment he had expected, but a grave, almost troubled glance. Thol Orr got up and motioned politely toward his chair. Thayn sat down, facing Wilson with her clear profile toward Hammond and the others. Before anyone said anything, she spoke to Wilson in a low voice.

"I beg you to listen to the warnings I've already given you. You cannot reach Althar. You will surely perish if you try—all of you."

"You mean, I suppose, that this ship will be detonated?" said Wilson.

Thayn said wearily, "You cannot approach the Trifid without being detected by Vramen radar. And please do not cherish the illusion that my presence here will keep the Vramen officer who challenges you from doing his duty."

Wilson glanced at Thol Orr, and the Algolian spoke

gently to Thayn. "Suppose we have a way to get past that obstacle?"

"There is no way. Surely you know that if you try to remove the detonator, it will automatically explode."

"We know that," Thol Orr said. "But there is a way, nevertheless. You can't stop us, Marden. You may as well help us."

"Help you reach Althar?" she said incredulously.

Thol Orr continued to press her with questions, and Thayn gave more and more scornful answers. To Hammond the questions did not seem to make too much sense. They wandered afield, and he began to think that Thol Orr was a bit stupid in his examination.

But suddenly Thayn looked intently at Thol Orr and said, "There is some purpose behind these irrelevant questions. I have nothing more to say."

Wilson nodded to Lund. "Take her back to her cabin, Gurth."

When she had gone Thol Orr sat down in the chair again and Wilson asked him anxiously,

"Have you got it?"

"I think so," said Thol Orr. "But it was a close thing. Marden's no fool. Another minute and she'd have guessed what we were up to."

"And what the devil *were* you up to?" Quobba asked.

Thol Orr went to the metal wall of the cabin a few yards in front of his chair. He slid aside a small plate in the wall, invisible till then. In a recess behind it was mounted a compact, camera-like device.

"This is a stereovideo-tape recorder," he said. "I brought it along from the guard base at Kuum, figuring we'd surely need it for this purpose."

"For what purpose?"

"It has been making a stereovideo tape of every word Marden said. I asked her leading questions so that she would speak certain words in her answer. Now, we'll edit the tape, cut it into separate words and piece the words into a new tape which will show Marden speaking a certain sentence."

For the next few days Thol Orr spent all his waking hours in the communic room of the ship. Hammond could not understand all that he was doing. The editing and re-shuffling of the stereovideo tape he could comprehend, and the fact that Thol Orr was setting up a projector so that the ship telaudio transmitter would present the tape as a live speech by Thayn Marden.

"It should work if there's only a formal challenge," said Thol Orr, and added worriedly, "The danger is if extensive questions are asked, for no pre-recorded tape can carry on a conversation."

"And if we pass the challenge?" Hammond asked.

The Algolian pointed to a complex of apparatus in one corner. "The challenge will come from Althar. That's a very powerful and sensitive direction-finder. From the Vramen telaudio call it should give us a fix on just where Althar lies inside the Trifid."

Six days after Hammond's awakening in the ship, it passed completely around a dark cloud that lay like a gloomy curtain across their way.

The Trifid lay before them.

It had been impressive enough in the astronomical photographs that Hammond had seen back in the Twentieth Century, when it was called the Trifid Nebula. But from this distance it was stunning.

Great star-clouds glittered all around them, the swarms of suns that in the Sagittarius region of the Milky Way made brilliant the summer nights of faraway Earth. But beyond all these loomed a vastness of light, glowing like a furnace in which stars were forged, stretching across whole parsecs of space. Groups of double and multiple stars shone from within that far-flung nebulosity, some of them fiercely bright and others dim and muffled. And the whole shining mass of the Trifid was riven by three great cracks that were themselves light-years in width and that formed clear roads into the inconceivable interior.

The light of the Trifid glowed upon their faces as they peered from the pilot-room, Tammas at the controls and Jon Wilson and Quobba and Iva crowded beside Hammond. Hammond wondered if they felt the same awe as he did. For now, with the Trifid looming gigantic before them and dwarfing the stars to dust, it seemed to him that they were impiously approaching the very throne of God.

Wilson's taut voice broke the spell. "We could get a challenge any time. I'll make sure Thol is ready."

Hammond turned and followed him out of the pilot-room. He didn't want to look any longer at the Trifid. He thought that if he did, all his courage would run out of him.

In the communic room, Thol Orr nodded calmly. "It's all ready. Remember, no one is to speak or get within range of the telaudio transmitter eye."

They waited. The generators droned and the ship went on and on. They looked at the telaudio screen and nothing happened.

The telaudio buzzed sharply and Hammond started violently.

"That'll be it," said Wilson. "Be sure—"

"Quiet," said Thol Orr, in the tone of one who soothes a nervous child. He touched a switch.

In the telaudio receiver screen appeared the head of a man. He was a handsome young man, and beyond him was a background of apparatus unfamiliar to Hammond. He looked like any other pleasant, efficient young man. He was a Vramen and Hammond hated him.

"State the identity of your ship," he said.

Thol Orr touched another switch. The stereovideo projector came on. It threw, right in front of the transmitter-eye of the telaudio, a life-sized three-dimensional image whose solidarity and reality made Hammond catch his breath. The image was Thayn Marden.

The Marden-image spoke quickly. "Returning for special consultation. There are none but Vramen on this ship."

The speech was only faintly jerky. It should convince anybody, Hammond thought. He hoped it would convince the Vramen in the screen. If it didn't, the man had only to press a key and they would never know what happened to them.

Chapter 13

IN THE screen, the eyes of the young Vramen man lighted with pleasure. He said,

"We'll be glad to see you here again, Thayn. It has been a long time. Proceed."

And the screen went dark.

Thol Orr turned a switch and the vividly real stereovideo image of Thayn disappeared. And Hammond suddenly became conscious that there had been an iron band around his chest which had now loosened. They looked at each other with relief and triumph, and Wilson said,

"Well done, Thol. We foxed the Vramen this time!"

Thol Orr shook his head. "Not for very long. Remember, the Vramen will now expect Marden to arrive at their Althar base, wherever it may be. When she doesn't, they'll take alarm and start searching."

"By that time, we'll hope to have got somewhere," muttered Wilson. He went over to North Abel, the younger Algolian, who during all this time had been hunched over the complex of directional receivers in the corner of the room. "Did you get a fix, North?"

"Yes, I got one. I'll have to work out the bearings before I plot it."

Presently the small navigation room was crowded as Lund, Abel, Wilson and Thol Orr all hung over a table. Hammond looked on from behind them, but could not make the slightest sense out of the mass of symbols and graphs they were studying.

"That's it," said Abel finally. "Unless they were using a relay point, that's the direction of Althar."

They all looked at Wilson. He tugged at his lip nervously, staring down at the sheets of symbols. Finally he said,

"This is the way we have to take. The Vramen may have some better way but we don't know it. At least, this takes us in along a rift a good way before we have to cut through the nebula."

Lund's hard face became a trifle more bleak. "Cutting through the nebula will be rough."

"It will," said Wilson. "It is also the only chance we have."

Hammond found the opportunity to ask Thol Orr, "Why will the nebula be rough going? I always thought that nebular matter was so tenuous it was hardly there."

Thol Orr nodded. "That's right. The Trifid looks like a fiery mass but actually it's all reflection of light from the many stars inside it. The dust of which it's composed is less dense than any hard vacuum we use in a laboratory. It wouldn't bother the ship."

"Then what will?"

"Magnetic fields. The clouds of dust in the Trifid are in motion, swirling and colliding with each other. The collision of these clouds creates the most intense kind of magnetic fields, constantly changing. You can imagine how those fields will affect our photon-drive."

Time went by and the ship still droned toward the Trifid. Hammond ate and slept, and this time he had no fear of the nightmare that had haunted him. Nor did that nightmare come, yet when he awoke he remembered a different and strangely disturbing dream. It seemed to him that he had again held Thayn Marden in his arms and that suddenly she had laughed at him and vanished, and he realized that she was only a stereovideo image and had never existed at all.

He wondered how she felt, locked up in her little cabin. Was she scared? He doubted that. She was an arrogant and unhuman witch, but she had courage. He supposed that she was very angry. He hoped she was. He asked himself why the devil he was thinking about her at all, and got up out of his bunk and went forward.

The vista in the pilot-room viewplate hit him like a blow. The Trifid walled all the heavens in front of them, a glowing glory of inconceivable dimensions. Stars and star-groups burned here and there in it, their reflected radiance lighting the tenuous dust. The great black rifts that had been visible even from Earth were now colossal chasms of darkness through this continent of light. The ship was heading toward the mouth of one of those mighty cracks.

Shau Tammas turned his yellow face from the pilot-chair and grinned. "Pretty, isn't it? Only the damned Vramen would want to live in a place like this."

After a while the firmament on either side of them was walled with light as the ship crawled into the vast dark chasm. By this time Rab Quobba was back at the controls, and their course was close alongside one of the glowing walls.

They moved along the coasts of light like a mote beside a sun, past fiery-glowing capes that could have held the whole Solar System, past great bays of darkness that ran far back into the nebula. Hammond's mind quailed. He was still a child of the Twentieth Century, of the little Earth, and this monster cloud was no place for man. The light of it beat upon the faces of Iva and Tammas and Abel, peering with him, and he saw awe in their eyes too.

Jon Wilson came and said, "You'd better strap in. Our direction-line takes us into the nebula soon, and we'll have to run that on autopilot."

Iva went away but Quobba pointed to one of the empty chairs and Hammond sat down and strapped in.

Lund's voice came from the annunciator. "Autopilot."

"Autopilot it is, and I hope the blasted calcs know their business," said Quobba.

He closed a circuit and then turned and gave Hammond a

wry grin. "Here's where you get an advanced lesson. Running any nebula is tricky, but the Trifid—"

His words were drowned out. The computers back in the calc-room, whose relays could think faster than any human being, had taken over. They had been given an objective, the line deep in the cloud that was the way to Althar. They made their computations in a few seconds of whirring and clicking. They spoke, not in audible speech but in electric impulses that gave imperious orders to the autopilot mechanism. The generators deep in the ship, forewarned of the need for a greater power, droned loud. The autopilot took the ship and, at a speed that just stopped short of the threshold of human endurance, flung it right at the glowing wall.

Hammond saw them coming, those precipices of light that went forever up into starry space. He braced himself for an impact that he knew would not come. He was right. There was no impact when they hit the nebula. There was only light all around them, not so fiery or bright now that they were in it but more a moony glow. They droned and raced through a softly-lit limbo that seemed not to change at all until finally the muffled fires of a triple sun shone vaguely ahead of them and to the right. And of a sudden the ship shivered and then quieted, and then shivered again and again. The great magnetic tides of the nebula abruptly took hold of the ship and carried it away for an instant like a chip on a millrace, and Hammond saw the whole vague vista of glowing nebula and flaring triple suns spinning around and around.

The generators droned louder still. The autopilot stuttered furiously. The mindless brain of the computer had detected the change in course and was instantly giving its orders. The ship broke free of the magnetic field that held it and shot away from the three suns, and then was gripped again. It seemed certain to Hammond that the crazy interaction of intersecting fields was going to end up by dragging them into one of those stars that soon loomed frighteningly big and

126

bright through the glow, two of them warm yellow and one a hot blue-white.

But the computer fought the nebula. Where man had not the quickness of thought to act, the thing that man had made acted for him, did battle for him. Hammond thought that he had been right and that there was no place here for man, that only a mechanical intelligence that had no nerves or feelings could fight the blind vast forces of the cloud.

The three suns dropped behind them. There was a deceptively quiet period. Then Hammond saw the telltale lights on the control panel blinking furiously, like little bright mouths opening and closing, crying soundlessly of death and danger near them.

He could not read those telltales but Quobba could, and he groaned. "Drift all around us—that's all we needed!"

The computer had been until now their champion. Hammond thought of it with a dim reverence. But it seemed that it had had too much to bear for it appeared now to go crazy.

It threw the ship every which way in the next few minutes. They were hurled against their straps and the blurred view in the scanners whirled in dizzying fashion. Then for the first time Hammond heard an actual sound of impact, a crash of hail on the hull, hitting the gyrating ship now on one side and then on the other.

Over the full-throated roar of the generators, Quobba yelled reassuringly to Hammond. "It's the drift—little dust-aggregates. Our radar-warning system keeps us from ramming anything big."

The warnings were also going to break them into little pieces, Hammond thought, as the ship twisted and turned and dodged to avoid the drift. He was sore from the pressure of the straps by the time the telltales stopped their flashing.

And still they droned on through the nebula. Far-off stars shone glimmering in the glowing dust like drowned fires, and dropped away. Again the suck of a magnetic tide drew them away, and again the computer with a sublime pig-headedness brought them back on course.

Hammond slept in his straps, finally. Not physical but mental and nervous exhaustion overpowered him, after what he had seen.

He was awakened by a change of timbre in the droning that pervaded the ship. He rubbed his eyes, which felt tired and bleary. There was no wild motion now, but something was different. He looked inquiringly at Quobba.

"We're slowing down," said Quobba. "Caught a star ahead on radar. It has a planet—we think it may be Althar."

The name snapped Hammond to full wakefulness. He peered eagerly forward. There was the moony glow, and there was something in it dead center ahead of them, a vague spot of brighter light.

Lund and Wilson came and peered sharply. The spot of light brightened very slowly in the glimmering haze, and Hammond thought that they must have decelerated quite a bit before he awoke.

Wilson said, "I've got Thol and North scanning for drift. Any debris in space near that sun will give us some cover from their radar."

North Abel came hurrying into the pilot-room with a sheet of paper in his hand. "Here's the data on the nearest drift."

Wilson looked at the sheet and then handed it to Quobba. "Not too bad. If you can jockey into that stuff it ought to hide us."

The haze of the nebula was thinning out ahead of them. Of course, Hammond thought. The gravitational field of a star would keep space clear of the tiny particles for a distance around it, since the star would sweep them up as it moved. And because there was clear space not far ahead, the star there came brighter to his eyes. It looked weirdly iridescent, opalescent, many-colored, and that he supposed was because he saw it through the thinning haze. He heard the occasional rattle of tiny particles of dust-aggregate against the hull, but none of them paid any attention to that.

They were all of them, Wilson, Quobba, Abel and Lund,

staring ahead as fixedly as Hammond himself. And now as the ship rushed through the last of the haze, the solitary sun ahead came clear to their eyes. It spun here in the depths of the Trifid, a sun with a single planet that looked a little smaller than Earth, and that planet might well be Althar, desired by all Hoomen for so long. Yet in this moment, not one of them looked at the planet. They looked at the star.

"By all the gods of space," muttered Quobba. "I never saw a sun like *that*."

Nobody answered him. Nobody could answer, least of all Hammond. All he could do was stare.

It had been no trick of refraction that had made this star look strange. Its weird opalescence was even more pronounced now that they looked upon its naked glory. It appeared to have no single hue, but red, green, violet, and golden yellow spun in its light like the writhing colors of a huge fire-opal. It was uncanny, hypnotic, as it spun here at the heart of the nebula, bathing its little planet in coruscating and changing light.

Wilson broke the silence. "I thought I knew all star-types, but this one—"

"There's never *been* a type like this," said North Abel. His pallid face was slack and stunned as he stared. He turned and almost ran. "I'm going to tell Thol about this."

Hammond looked at the others. "Is that planet Althar?"

A deep glow came into Wilson's eyes. "It could be."

Quobba looked at him inquiringly. "Then we land on it?"

"Yes. But we have to stay under cover of the drift as long as we can. Gurth, you set it up on the computer."

Lund went out. Hammond remained with Wilson and the Vegan, staring at the opalescent star. Its weird glory deepened as they drew nearer to it. Watching the continual flux of color in its light, Hammond felt more than a little mesmerized. This was not like a star of his own galaxy. It was as alien as though it had come into being to illumine unimaginably strange worlds in some remote galaxy far across the cosmos. When Iva Wilson came in and looked at it, she uttered a low exclamation.

"It's beautiful—but somehow frightening."

"Thol wants you," said North Abel to Wilson. "Right away. He's found out something about that star."

"What?"

Abel looked as though his eyes were popping out of his head from excitement, but he was making an effort to appear calm.

"He'll tell you himself. He wants you right away."

Wilson gave him a sharp glance and then turned and went. Iva and Hammond followed, the girl with a wondering look and Hammond with a sudden excitement setting his own pulses to leaping.

Thol Orr was in the navigation room and as they entered he turned from the spectroscopic instrument he had been poking toward the opalescent star. Hammond had never seen the Algolian look like this. His hands were trembling and his face had a stiff, strange look. He said,

"You know I was a radiation expert? And that I was sent to Kuum because I was nosing around too near the Trifid, studying a flicker of unusual radiation?"

"Yes, we know that," said Wilson impatiently. "What I want to know is more about this star. Is it the sun of Althar?"

"I'm trying to tell you," Thol Orr said. "The unprecedented radiation I tried to trace years ago—it's coming from this star, in great strength. And it's a kind of radiation never found before."

He paused, apparently trying to put into words something difficult to communicate. With astonishment, Hammond realized suddenly that Thol Orr was afraid.

"It's been postulated that there could be radiation far higher in frequency than the so-called cosmic rays. Theory has indicated that electromagnetic vibrations of such high frequency might have incalculable effects on human tissue. And—it is that kind of radiation that is pouring out of the star."

Wilson said, "Suppose you're right, what does it—"

He stopped suddenly. A strange pallor came over his face. He looked at the opalescent star and then back again at the Algolian.

Thol Orr nodded. "That's what I mean. I think that you won't have to look for the Vramen secret of life on Althar. I think the secret is there."

And he pointed at the alien glory of the star.

Chapter 14

SINCE THE dawn of eternity, the mighty cloud of the Trifid had guarded a secret. What strange chemistry had created it, what unimaginable blind interplay of cosmic forces, were beyond human thinking. In the deepest recesses of the great nebula a thing had been born that was like no other known in the cosmos. And then, two thousand years ago, eight thousand years after the conquest of space, the ships of men had come questing and nosing into the nebula and men had found the secret.

Had found—the star?

No, Hammond thought. It's too monstrous a violation of the familiar, too incredible. Whatever they found in here that gave them unending life and made them the Vramen, it can't be this.

Or can it?

Thol Orr was talking. He had been talking now for some minutes, and there was a passion in his voice that Hammond had never heard there before. The talk was of radiation and of tissue, of what high-frequency energy could do to cells, of how it might stimulate and powerfully strengthen the regenerative process, the power of a cell to renew itself, so that the cell would not age or die. And again and again Thol pointed to the opalescent star, and in his eyes as he looked at it was the hungering joy of a lover who finds his dream.

Jon Wilson flung up his hand for silence. "Let us think! If this thing is as you believe—"

Quobba, his eyes wide and stunned, exclaimed, "If it is, the radiation of the star—just the sunlight from it—can give us all indefinite life. Make us Vramen!"

It is impossible, said Hammond's mind. These men have followed a fierce desire so long that now they are embracing a chimera. But though his reason said that, his eyes looked at the star and his heart cried out, *Life, life, life!*

Of a sudden the whole ship was full of calling voices and running feet, men and women crowding to get into the pilot-room, to get to the scanners and look out. Either Abel or someone else had been babbling and there was an excitement that was rising to hysteria. All your life you lived with the knowledge of death hanging over you like a sword, and as long as everyone else died in time it was a thing you accepted. But to live and age and die in the same universe with other men and women like yourself who neither aged nor died, to pass down into the darkness while the few, the undying went on and on, and now at last to work and dare and see the great flaring fountain of undying life before your very eyes, it was for all these people an even more soul-shaking thing than it was for Hammond.

Discipline was dissolving into hysteria and the ship would be a madhouse within minutes. But not for nothing was Wilson their chosen leader. His voice rose and he ordered them, cursed them and practically beat them back down from the heights of their exalted excitement.

"There's nothing sure about any of this yet," he shouted. "You hear me—nothing! The radiation of the star may be the secret of life, or it may not. If you act like children, we'll never have a chance to find out. Remember what's down in our hull."

That sobered them, that reference to the Vramen detonator that at any instant could blow them to atoms. Death

132

seemed a more terrible thing now that unending life might be within their grasp.

"Get them back down below," he told Lund. "And bring Marden up here, quick."

"We're almost out of the drift cover," Quobba warned. "What now?"

Hammond looked ahead at the greenish little planet that swung in the rays of the glittering star. So did Wilson, and his deep eyes glowed with determination.

"Hit straight for the planet," he said.

"Minute we come out of the drift, the Vramen on that world will radar us," warned Quobba.

"Let them. They'll still think it's Marden's ship coming in—for a while yet."

The computer had already calculated the flight pattern, and the ship went ahead fast. It was not on autopilot now, and Hammond saw Quobba's big hands twitching and clenching as he touched the controls from time to time. The generators droned loud again.

Thayn came into the little room, ahead of Gurth Lund. She did not at first spare Hammond, or any of them, a glance. Her eyes fixed on the scanner, on the stunning view of the opalescent star and its little world. Her white face became composed and expressionless.

"It's Althar, isn't it?" said Wilson.

She looked at him then, but she did not answer.

"Too late for silence, Marden!" said Wilson. "We're going to land there anyway."

Her face became very white, and when she spoke her voice was almost a whisper.

"Don't do it. I beg of you, turn and leave here. Now, at once."

Lund laughed. Thol Orr pressed forward and asked her eagerly, "The high-frequency radiation of the star there—it *is* the secret, isn't it?"

Thayn looked at him, and then at Wilson, and then, suddenly, at Hammond. He thought that there was a shadow of agony in her eyes, and something in her expression chilled him. Finally she said,

"Yes."

A long breath exhaled from Wilson, the sigh of a man who all his life has struggled up a mountain and now at last can see the summit.

"How long does it take?" Thol Orr asked her. "How much exposure to the stellar radiation, to make our bodies like yours?"

She did not turn her gaze from Hammond's face as she answered. "Many days. Too many. You will not live that long, if you land on Althar."

And then she suddenly turned from Hammond and her gaze swept them all, her voice rising in passionate appeal.

"Don't do it. You are grasping for life, and you don't know yet what goes with it. That radiation is a dreadful biological snare. If you expose yourselves to it too long—"

"Please, Marden," interrupted Jon Wilson in a cutting voice, "don't try to frighten us like children. If the radiation had any deleterious effects, you Vramen wouldn't have lived so long."

Thayn's shoulders sagged a little. "Hopeless," she murmured. "It's why we Vramen have never told you the truth. We knew it was hopeless, that you'd never believe."

"At least," said Hammond, "we could hear what she has to say about it."

Lund turned fiery eyes on him. "That's what I would expect from you. I told them you couldn't be trusted, now or ever."

Tension made Hammond's own temper flare. "Listen, you damned well wouldn't have been here if it hadn't been for me!"

Jon Wilson roared at both of them like an angry old lion. "No more of that! By God, I'll have no quarrels now."

He turned back to Thayn. "Where is the main Vramen center on this planet?"

She said, "It is in the high mountains in the north polar

region of Althar. If you land at all, it must be there. Nowhere else on Althar will you be safe."

"Safe?" said Lund, and laughed again. "Oh, yes, safe in the arms of the Vramen."

"You don't understand!" she said. "We Vramen control only that limited north polar region. Almost all the rest of Althar is dominated by another race, the Third Men. You must not land where they can reach you."

Lund said violently, "What is the good of listening to all these lies? Of course she's trying to fob us off."

Thayn made a final appeal. "You won't land at Sharanna—at our Vramen center?"

"Are we fools?" said Wilson.

She looked at them, and her eyes came to rest on Hammond's face. Then she murmured, "It makes little difference then. We shall not live long. Goodbye, Kirk Hammond."

And she was gone with Tammas, and her *Goodbye, Kirk Hammond* left a troubled echo in Hammond's ears. Lund glared at him and then said to Wilson,

"You know what she means, that we won't live long."

Wilson nodded curtly. "It's obvious. The Vramen must have radar locked on us right now. If we set down anywhere but at that base of theirs, they'll suspect something wrong and blow the ship."

Quobba turned, and there was a fine film of sweat on his massive face. "So?"

"So," said Wilson, "ram straight in as though heading for the north polar region. Then, as we're coming in, do some freak spins and fall-offs, and set down suddenly. It'll look as though we're having mechanical trouble."

Hammond asked doubtfully, "You think that'll keep them from blowing the ship?"

"There's a chance," said Wilson, uncheeringly. "It seems that they'd try to call us first, maybe send out an assistance party."

"And if they find us?"

"They'll find trouble. We'll get out of the ship fast, with

everything we can get out of it. We'll wear rayproof turbans, and if the Vramen come after us with hypno-amplifiers they'll do no good. We have the shockers we brought from Kuum, we can stand them off."

"For how long?" asked Thol Orr skeptically.

"Long enough, maybe," answered Wilson. "We might have help. If the Vramen have enemies here, those enemies could be our friends. You heard Marden talk of a race she called the Third Men."

"A lie to frighten us into the arms of the Vramen," said Lund contemptuously.

"Maybe," said Wilson. "Yet back on Earth, remember what she told Hammond, 'And even if you passed the Vramen—' There was an implication there of others beside the Vramen at Althar. Who knows what other race beside man has found this world, this star of life?"

It was a thought that had not occurred to Hammond and it gave him a shock. There was something staggering about the possibility that from far away, perhaps even from galaxies beyond this one, other races might have come to this star to seek unending life. A great magnet drawing peoples human and unhuman from far away, like moths flitting around a candle, settling upon Althar, struggling jealously with each other . . .

The driving voice of Wilson swept such wild speculations out of his mind.

"We have to go on the assumption that the Vramen will detonate this ship soon," Wilson was saying. "Everything must be ready for disembarkation the moment we land. I want everything possible to be taken out of the ship—all the auxiliary atomic generators and tools, all the emergency repair equipment, as well as all weapons, tools, batteries and rations. Get it ready, Gurth—and hurry!"

There began a buzz of feverish preparations in the ship, with Lund and Thol Orr designating what must be made ready for rapid unloading. Wrenches clanged as men hastily unbolted machines the very purpose of which was a mystery to Hammond. Sweating men skidded them toward the cargo ports, and others under Lund's direction rigged improvised power-winch equipment to get the heavy items out when they landed. Hammond found himself with Abel carrying flat cartons of food-capsules which Iva Wilson brought out of a storeroom. There was a hurrying and crowding in all the corridors, and an echoing of excited voices that rose even above the drone of the generators.

Iva asked him, as he took still another carton from her, "What did Thayn Marden say?"

"A lot of things. Most of them intended to frighten us away from Althar."

She looked at him and unexpectedly she said, "Listen to her when she warns you of anything, Kirk. About the rest of us she may not care but I don't think she wants you to die."

He was startled. "Iva, you're crazy if you're implying—"

He got no farther than that. Air roared suddenly loud outside the hull, and then the annunciators throughout the ship bawled,

"Strap in, everyone!"

There was a scramble for the recoil-chairs. Hammond and Iva got two in the crew-room and then twisted their necks to stare up at the scanner in the wall.

It showed the view ahead, the sunlit side of the planet looming up across the screen. There were no seas on it but the rolling surface was rough with forests of some kind. They were dark green except for slashes of pure yellow that made Hammond think of the New Mexico mountains in the fall, with the aspens golden against the pines. The surface of the planet tilted sharply in the screen and then the ship seemed to stand on its tail and fall off in a dizzying roll.

The straps around Hammond cut into him and he heard a dismayed exclamation from Iva. They were in a spin, going down, and he wondered if Quobba was merely carrying out his orders to make it seem the ship was crashing, or whether this was a real crash. He thought it was real, this was too wild a spin to be a fake. The air roared louder and in the scanner he could glimpse the forest rushing up toward them, a thick forest of grotesquely lumpy dark-green growths. There was a crackling and crashing outside the ship and Hammond thought, It's a crazy way to die. Then there was a bump and that was followed by the most breathtaking thing of all.

Silence. No sound, no movement, for the first time since they had left Kuum.

The annunciators instantly shattered the silence. "Outside, everyone! Get the equipment out!"

Hammond helped Iva out of her straps and they ran, with others joining them to crowd the corridors, down toward the cargo-ports. The ports were already swinging open and outside there was a blaze of blinding sunlight slanting on tall, strange-looking clumps of green. The air swirled in, warm and light and dry.

Quickly the holds inside the cargo-ports became an organized madhouse of activity and noise. The gangways were run out, and men hastened to set up the power-equipment to winch the big atomic generators and other heavy machinery out of the ship. Others, including Hammond and Iva and Abel, carried loads of supplies out and well away from the ship and set them down in an improvised dump that was located on the side of a low ridge. Only when Hammond was running back to the ship for another load had he time to glance even at the weird forest that rose around them. Jon Wilson, out beside the ship, kept driving them.

"Faster! The ship can blow any moment! Get everything up to the dump—don't put down anything nearer the ship!"

A Vramen somewhere on this world could press a key and they would all be nothing. That knowledge spurred them, and the winches screaked and men bawled and sweated and the heavier machines moved out with brutish stolidity. And finally, they all stood amid the heaps of their frantic salvage, all out of the ship and able for the first time to catch their breath and look around them.

All about them rose the green clumps. They were not trees, they were mosses like gigantic cushions, towering twenty and thirty feet high and more than that in diameter. Between the huge moss-clumps grew a carpet of dark moss in which here and there were areas of true grass that was bright yellow in color. Hammond looked wonderingly at the colorless sky. The blaze of the setting opal sun was hidden from him by the clump beside him, but its rays twitched and quivered in the heavens like a daytime aurora. No birds or even insects moved in this somber moss-forest. No sound broke the deep and brooding silence as they stood, between fear and rapture, on the world of their desire.

Chapter 15

NIGHT LAY over Althar, but it was like no night that Hammond had ever seen before. There was no moon in the sky, and no stars. Instead the whole heavens were a glowing sheet, a nebula sky that shed a glimmering, almost shadowless radiance down upon the huge dark mosses. The Hoomen were gathered in a tight group beside their dump of machines and supplies, and since the sun set an hour before they had shown no lights. Some of them, armed with shockers, walked to and fro on watchful guard. Others slept.

Hammond could not sleep. Neither could Thayn Marden. He looked to where she sat at a little distance from him. Behind her and quite close to her sat Shau Tammas, and he knew that the monkey-faced little Mizarian kept his shocker trained constantly upon her. Hammond could see the white blur of her face in the eldritch glow. He wished he could talk to her. He decided he would talk to her, and the devil with Lund and Wilson's orders.

He stood up. The whole world blazed to a blinding white

light that lit up startled faces and towering mosses, and there was a clap of thunder and a wave of hot air hit Hammond from behind.

He staggered, retaining his balance and trying to turn around fast. A chorus of astonished cries broke as the flare and the thunder died.

"The ship!" yelled Quobba's bass voice.

Swinging around, Hammond saw a column of steam arising in the middle distance where the ship had rested. A breath of super-hot air still eddied around him.

Jon Wilson had leaped to his feet and run a few steps forward but now he stopped and his stern voice rang above the babble.

"Stay back! The Vramen have detonated the ship. We expected that."

A cold feeling went up Hammond's back. That could so easily have happened when they were in the ship, at any time since they had first approached the Trifid. His nerves were shaken by it, and it made him suddenly hate the Vramen more than ever to realize that they had that power of life and death over every ship in the galaxy.

Wilson turned and went back to Thayn. She was standing up, and in the moony glow her face was unreadable in expression, to Hammond. Wilson asked her harshly,

"Your friends did that—why did they blow it instead of coming to your assistance?"

Thayn said, "My people do not come into this part of Althar. It is too dangerous. I tried to tell you."

"Oh, yes," sneered Lund. "The Third Men. The bogle that was to frighten us into the hands of the Vramen."

"I think," said Thayn, "that the Third Men are coming now. At Sharanna, my people would be watching on the radar. If they detected hostile fliers searching for this ship, they'd detonate it at once." Her voice had a hopeless quality in it, and then it rose in a passionate appeal. "For the last time, I beg you—destroy the metal and machines you have here! If these fall into the hands of the Third Men—"

140

"Naturally you would like us to be without weapons or equipment of any sort," interrupted Wilson sourly. He turned and raised his voice. "All of you keep sharp watch and have your shockers handy. But don't use them unless I say so."

Hammond had one of the little stunning tubes. He didn't think much of it as a weapon if a real fight was coming up, and he said so.

"There need not be any fight," said Wilson. "There won't be, if I can prevent it. Whoever these other people are, if they're enemies of the Vramen it stands to reason they could be our friends. I don't want anyone getting panicky and spoiling the chance of that."

"Listen!" said Iva.

A sound was coming out of the glowing heavens, a shrill piping that was discontinuous and very thin, now fading away and then coming more strongly than before.

"Fliers," said Thayn. "They would have seen the flare of the ship going."

"Watch her," said Wilson to Shau Tammas. "Don't look at anything else but her, no matter what happens."

He hurried off with Lund and they stood with the Hoomen clustered around them, beside one of the giant mosses, staring up into the sky in which the piping was now changing to a steady whistling.

Thayn looked at Hammond. "You should be very happy," she said. "You have done what you dreamed of doing, what Hoomen for centuries have dreamed of doing. You have reached Althar, and in time the radiation of the star will make you all undying as we Vramen are and you will be happy then, just as we are."

There was a shocking bitterness in her words. It grated painfully on Hammond's nerves, and he stepped closer to her.

"Thayn, what is it? What are you expecting?"

She made a mirthless sound. "Nothing. I expect nothing at all. I am merely telling more Vramen lies." She paused

141

for a moment, and Hammond heard the whistling across the sky screeching louder and lower. Thayn said, "Your new friends are coming. Run to them, greet them. For they will surely help you against the hated Vramen!"

The screeching roar blotted out anything Hammond might have wanted to say, and he looked up and saw four long slim shapes flash swiftly above them, standing out black against the glowing sky. The whistling rose to maniacal heights, and then fell off as the four fliers banked sharply around on their stubby wings and came back. This time one was much lower than the other three. The three made another straight pass overhead but the single craft swept down to land out of sight behind the ridge.

They waited then, their shockers in their hands, their tension rising. No one came and nothing happened, except that the three fliers whistled back overhead again. Waiting, listening, peering, Hammond felt the deepening of an unease that had been in him since he had heard Thayn's bitter words. He went to Wilson, who stood a little in front of them facing the ridge, and spoke to him.

"I don't like it. They could be taking up position all around us while we wait here," said Hammond.

"There will be no fighting, there is no need for it," Wilson said inflexibly.

And then the Hooman leader stepped forward a little farther and called aloud, his voice rolling out into the lonesome night, the great dark moss-clumps brooding beneath the glowing sky.

"We are friends!"

There was no answer for moments, no sound except the whistling scream of the other fliers circling around somewhere overhead. Then from over the low ridge, a cold, strong voice repeated the last word upon a rising note.

"Friends?"

"We are Hoomen, not Vramen," said Wilson loudly. "We don't know who you are but we take it you are not Vramen either."

This time the answer came more quickly in the same universal galactic language, and it seemed to Hammond that there was a tone of irony in the chill, precise voice.

"No, we are not Vramen," it said. "Oh, no! The Vramen are no friends of ours."

"Nor of ours," Wilson assured quickly. "They hunted us, they tried to keep us from coming to this world, they destroyed our ship. We have one of them prisoner here."

"A Vramen prisoner?" The counter-question came quickly as a wolf-snap.

"Yes. So if you are enemies of the Vramen, you cannot be *our* enemies."

There was a pause, and in the strain of the moment Hammond thought he heard low whisperings from beyond the little ridge. Then the chill voice spoke clearly.

"I am Mar Kann of the Third Men, and I come to you without weapons. There is no reason why we cannot be friends."

Hammond, peering with the others, saw a man come up from behind the low ridge and stand upon it. He was a dark, stark figure against the glowing sky, big but completely human in outline. He walked toward them and now they saw that this man was fully seven feet in height, superbly statured. He wore a close-fitting dark tunic, his arms and legs bare. His head was bare too and his completely hairless skull gleamed in the soft light as he came with long strides. Now they could see him clearly.

A woman among the Hoomen uttered a brief nervous sound that was half a giggle and half a scream. Rab Quobba exhaled his breath in a long gusty sigh. Iva had come to Hammond's side and her small hand dug suddenly into his arm.

Hammond felt shock himself. The first sight of the man's figure had swept away all his vague speculation about alien, unhuman beings who might have thronged to this star of life. He had felt relieved, but now he saw the man's face. It was a completely hairless face, the eyes browless and lashless. The features were regular and handsome, but the eyes were utterly without warmth or compassion. It was the cold, masklike face of an uncaring god.

The man stopped a few yards away from them, and stared. He was not staring at the Hoomen but at the heaped-up supplies and machines beyond them. He stood quite motionless for a long moment, and then his head moved and his gaze swept over them. Hammond felt that gaze like a physical impact.

"Let me see this Vramen prisoner," said the cold voice.

Wilson turned and nodded toward Thayn Marden, a little behind them. The eyes of Mar Kann fastened upon her. After a moment he said,

"I do not know her. I had hoped that she might be someone very dear to me."

"I was spared that shame," said Thayn, and though Hammond could not understand her meaning, the hatred and loathing in her voice were beyond mistaking.

"Witness the injustice of the Vramen," said Mar Kann in a bantering tone. "For all these ages they have hated us, whom they should love the most."

The irony was lost on Jon Wilson but one phrase caught him and his stern face became hungering as he repeated,

"For all these ages? Then you too—you Third Men—have unending life?"

"But of course," said the other. "It is a sorrow to the Vramen that it is so, but all who dwell under the rays of our sun live very long."

"Including the beloved children of the Third Men," said Thayn.

The reference was incomprehensible to Hammond but he saw that Mar Kann understood it for the ironic amusement left that unhumanly handsome face and his eyes shot a look of fiery hatred at Thayn. But again, Wilson clung to his lifelong purpose to the exclusion of all else.

"Then the rays of the star can give Hoomen unending life too?"

He hung tensely upon the answer and Hammond saw that all of them were eagerly listening. The momentary flash of anger left Mar Kann's face and he surveyed the Hoomen shrewdly.

"So that is why you have come to Althar," he murmured. "Ah, yes. Well, you have not come in vain. After some weeks' exposure to the rays of our sun your bodies will be changed in every cell, and sickness and aging will be cleansed from them." His voice rose, addressing them all. "You can help us, and we can help you. Come with us to Vonn—it is our chief city—and talk of these things."

Before anyone else could say anything, Thayn spoke rapidly "Don't trust the Third Men. What they really want is—"

"Be silent, woman," said Mar Kann, taking a step toward her and speaking in tones of ice.

Hammond saw Thayn glance at the Third Man and then he saw her face stiffen and change. Her voice trailed away, and a dull look came into her eyes. Her slim body seemed to sag, and she stood like a marionette without powers of speech or movement.

Hammond sprang forward. "What have you done to her?"

Mar Kann turned toward him, and Hammond felt the impact of those lashless eyes. "She is unharmed. I have merely silenced her by mental command."

"No hypnosis would work that fast," said Hammond angrily. "You used some weapon—"

Contempt came into the other's face. "Mental mastery of the Vramen is easy. Look at her. Yet these are the people who keep the Third Men prisoned on this world."

"Prisoned?" repeated Jon Wilson, amazed. "I don't understand—"

"It will all be explained to you in Vonn," said Mar Kann smoothly. "I am sure we can be allies. We do not need you people—but we do need some of these metals and machines you have here. They are of elements very scarce upon this world."

Wilson looked at him and then he swung around and spoke to all the staring Hoomen. "I say, we go! If these people are the enemies of the Vramen, that's enough."

"You choose wisely," nodded Mar Kann. "It will require more fliers than we have here to transport you and these valuable things. Wait, and I will call for more to come from Vonn."

He turned and strode back up over the ridge, was darkly outlined once more against the nebula sky, and went on down out of sight. The eyes of all except Hammond followed him.

Hammond had gone to Thayn. He took her hand, spoke to her. She made no answer and her eyes looked at him with a stunned, unseeing expression. Thol Orr came over and looked at her closely.

"I think she is all right, merely under post-hypnotic command," he said. "But—what kind of people are these who have such mental mastery over even the Vramen?"

Lund spoke angrily to Hammond. "You could have ruined our chances of alliance with these Third Men by your solicitude for this damned Vramen woman."

"I wonder," Hammond said, "just how equal an alliance we'll have with people to whom even the Vramen are inferiors."

Jon Wilson nodded nervously. "I thought of that. Yet the Vramen must be in some way their superiors, you heard what he said about the Vramen keeping them prisoned on this world. Well, without a ship we're prisoned here too, and we want to get back eventually and tell the secret of this star to the whole galaxy. So our best chance is to work with these Third Men."

There was a general murmur of agreement but it was not a hearty or enthusiastic one. And when Hammond stepped back, Quobba came up to him and said,

"Who the devil are these Third Men, anyway?"

Hammond shook his head. "I wish I knew. And I wish

I knew what Thayn was about to tell us—though maybe it would only have been a lie."

They had reached the guarded planet that Hoomen for centuries had dreamed of attaining, and yet it seemed to Hammond that they were enmeshed in darkening mysteries that took the joy out of their triumph. And though this was the planet of life that all men coveted, it seemed a brooding, silent, joyless world.

Quobba asked, "Did you see his hands?"

"His hands? Why, no," said Hammond. "He kept them down against his sides."

Quobba nodded. "I know, but I was close when he turned and I saw them. They were six-fingered. These people may look like humans, but they don't belong to our species at all."

Chapter 16

STANDING AT the window with the hot opalescent sunlight beating upon his face and his hands, Hammond wondered.

What will it be like to live indefinitely? How will I feel a hundred years from now? A thousand?

Take the idea into your mind. Turn it over and over, look at the shape of it from every side. It is impossible that Kirk Hammond of Earth is, barring accident, going to live practically forever. It is impossble but it is true. The sunlight beating on you is more than sunlight. It is the radiation of a star unique in the galaxy, perhaps in the whole cosmos, a star that is a gigantic generator of electromagnetic forces unknown elsewhere. Its invisible highest-frequency rays are at this moment searching every cell in your body, with a polarizing effect that in time will transform cytological structure completely. Each cell will acquire a regenerative power hitherto unknown in higher animals, will be able to repair the ravages of age or disease at once. In a few weeks, you will be transformed by the cumulative effect of this radiation. You will be, practically speaking, immortal.

Hammond, struggling with the hugeness of that thought, heard the voices of the others in the room only vaguely. They were still talking, there at the long table in the center of the room. They had been talking ever since the Hoomen had arrived in this city—Wilson and a dozen of the Hoomen with four of the Third Men. They had talked of some strange things in that time, but it was the final assurance of unending life that had made Hammond get up from the table and walk to this open window. He had to have time to take that in.

He looked out with half-unseeing eyes across the city of Vonn. It was a black cement city, set on the open yellow plain, its ebon color unrelieved by the glorious flood of light that streamed down from the opal sun. It was a small city but it looked stark and massive. Its buildings were almost all square in cross-section, arranged in a severely geometrical design around this massive central structure from whose window he looked. There were streets down there, and buildings that looked like factories or laboratories, and others that were certainly apartments. There was a paved plaza below in which were parked a score of the fliers. It was where they had landed when they had come here.

Hammond thought of those fliers. They had been a surprise to him. They were not of metal but of plastic, and they were not powered by atomic generators like nearly every other machine he had seen in the outer universe. Their propulsion was by means of jets and the chemical jet motor was of ceramic stuff, not metal. Looking down at them, he saw men and women moving between them on the plaza, and the square, shiny forms of several Mechs. He had met Mechs when they arrived, and he didn't like them.

Two fliers zoomed up as he watched, rising on vertical jets and then darting away. His eyes followed them but in a moment they were out of sight in the glittering blaze of sunlight, heading out over the vast moss-forest that surrounded the plain of the city. He wondered where they were going. He wondered where, ultimately, he was going himself.

"Hammond." It was Jon Wilson speaking and his voice was impatient, almost querulous. "Will you come back here?"

Hammond turned and went back to the table. It was of black plastic and so were the chairs, while the walls and ceiling of the room were of a pleasant gray. It occurred to Hammond that these people did not like colors, not in flowers, textiles, anything.

He sat down in his chair again. He hated to meet the cold probing gaze of the four men at the end of the table. He thought, the hell with them, look them in the eye. He did.

"It's hard to take it all in, isn't it?" said Holl Gormon pleasantly to him. "But your coming to Althar has precipitated a situation that has been long building, and there is a certain urgency. We want you to understand everything."

Holl Gormon was one of the directors of the Third Men. What that title meant, Hammond had not the faintest idea but he assumed that Gormon was high in whatever form of government these people had, and that Mar Kann and the other two men at the end of the table were also. It disturbed him that the four men looked so much alike. There were no age differences here to make identification easy. They all looked to be in strong youth or young-middle-age, they were all big men, they all had grave, cold faces. The Hoomen along the table, different in age, size, even in color, looked like a motley rabble beside them.

"You were saying," Jon Wilson said with an irritated glance at Hammond, "that you're willing for all the Hoomen in the galaxy to share in the secret of life."

"Yes," said Holl Gormon. "We have no desire to monopolize undying life. That is the Vramen's doing. Of course, it would be impossible to bring all the trillions of the galaxy here to Althar. But we feel sure the unique radiation of our sun could be duplicated artificially in time, and thus be extended to all your peoples."

Wilson's face became rapt. He said, "I don't care for myself. But if I could see that happen, see all human life extended—"

"It can be," said Gormon. "It will be. The long, jealous monopoly of the Vramen will surely be unlocked now. For your coming has brought the key."

He looked around their faces, and again Hammond felt a flinching at the impact of that chill gaze. It didn't make you feel easy when you were sure the man talking to you could dominate you hypnotically if he wanted to, just as Mar Kann had dominated Thayn. He wondered if Thayn was still under that influence. She had been left under a Hooman guard in one of the rooms assigned to them in this building, and Hammond had had no chance to see her.

"—and we Third Men are native to this world, born upon it, always an undying race since our beginning," Gormon was saying. "But we've never been able to leave this world, despite our great advances in scientific knowledge. For this is a world without metal."

And suddenly Hammond realized that he had not indeed seen a scrap of metal in use, not in the fliers or anywhere in this building.

"You mean, you've built this whole civilization of yours on a non-metallic basis?" said Thol Orr incredulously.

Gormon nodded. "We have had to. The peculiar non-metallic constitution of our sun, to which it owes its unique radiation, is duplicated in Althar, its planetary offspring. We have had to learn to use plastics, ceramics, cements, instead of metal. But one thing you cannot build without metal is a star-ship. You have to have metal for its frame, for its atomic generators and their fuel, for the magnetic enclosures necessary in fusion-power reactors. So we have had no star-ships. The only star-ships on this world are those in which the Vramen come and they land in only one place—their guarded base Sharanna in the northern mountains. And they never let us near that place for they have no intention of letting us go to the outer galaxy and tell the peoples there of the secret of life."

He paused and spread his hands out upon the table in a frank gesture.

"You see that I am being quite honest with you. The metals and atomics that you salvaged before your ship was blown are infinitely precious here. With them, we could start a process of element-building that would give us all the materials we lack. And with them, we could very quickly construct a weapon more powerful than all the weapons by which Sharanna dominates Althar."

Wilson leaned forward. "Let us be clear. For our equipment and our help, you offer what?"

"The secret of the star of life, to be taken to all the galaxy by star-ships we shall be able then to build," said Gormon promptly. "And protection, with the weapon we can forge, against the Vramen. For when they learn what we plan, you will need such protection!"

He stood up. "Think about that and talk it over among yourselves. Whatever your decision, you are our guests. We hope that you will be our allies also."

"I think you can count us as allies right now," Wilson said warmly.

Gormon said gravely, "That is good to hear. But still you will want to rest and to discuss the matter."

It was in effect a dismissal, though Gormon made it a courteous one by walking with them to the door. He said,

"There are many things we have to tell you yet, but they can wait a little. You are the first visitors we have ever had and every man and woman among us welcomes your coming."

The words reminded Hammond of something, of a puzzling taunt that Thayn Marden had flung at Mar Kann, and he asked,

"Men and women are all I've seen here—don't you have any children?"

Gormon turned swiftly and there was a sudden leaping blaze in his eyes. Hammond felt that look like a blow, but almost instantly it was gone, the man answered pleasantly,

"Our children do not live here but apart from us, for reasons of safety you will understand later."

He touched a plate and the door slid open. Outside it stood one of the Mechs. They had already learned that these things were merely cleverly designed, non-metallic robots actuated by chemical energy. There was nothing manlike about their shapes. This one was like the others Hammond had seen, a heavy black plastic cube four feet square, with jointed plastic arms furnished with pincer-hands for simple manipulation, the whole cube mounted on small wheels for movement. It had photoelectric lenses for purposes of rudimentary vision, and to provide depth-perception there were two of these set several inches apart. They gave the thing a goggling, glassy-eyed stare Hammond disliked.

"Conduct these people to Corridor Four-Two-Nine," said Gormon.

The Mech spoke metallically from a small grating in its side. "Please follow me."

It turned and rolled smoothly away. "It will take you back to your quarters," Gorman said. "We shall confer again when you've rested."

The Mech rolled down a wide corridor, turned into another, and then turned again into a moving, ascending ramp. Each time it changed direction it repeated, "Please follow me."

They came up into a corridor with open doors along it. The Mech stopped and spoke again.

"Your quarters. A nutrition-dispensary button is beside each door. The red button next to it will summon one of us."

The thing rolled back out of the corridor. Hammond followed Wilson and the others down the hall to the biggest room. Tammas, standing outside a closed door, greeted them as they passed.

"Any trouble?" Wilson asked.

The little Mizarian shook his head. "Not a bit. She hasn't said a word."

Hammond wondered. Was Thayn still under the influence of post-hypnotic command? He had not seen her on their arrival, Wilson had been careful to arrange that she and Hammond had made the trip in different fliers. He found it oppressive to think of her still staring blankly as when he had seen her last.

They went into the big common room of the suite, where the other Hoomen men and women awaited them. Iva ran anxiously to her father.

"Well?"

Jon Wilson looked around the anxious faces. "Everything is fine. These people here want to be our friends. They're as anxious as we are to leave this world and take the secret of life to the whole galaxy. The Vramen will try to prevent that, but we'll be allies together against the Vramen."

He added, after a moment, "They're so far beyond us in scientific ability that they wouldn't need us at all but for two things: they badly need the atomics and metals we saved out of the ship, and they want to learn more about the outer galaxy from us. I think we're lucky."

"I wonder," said Hammond, "just how lucky we are. These Third Men speak with contempt of the Vramen. How do they really feel toward us?"

Rab Quobba nodded uneasily. "The way they look at us gives me the creeps, somehow."

Wilson said angrily, "We've had the luck to find strong allies and you start finding fault with them. Maybe they don't think so much of us Hoomen. What of it? What matters is that with their help we can give undying life to all Hoomen."

Thol Orr had been listening silently, but now he spoke. "It will be a difficult task to reproduce the rays of the star artificially, to use all through the galaxy, but I believe it can be done in time."

Wilson nodded enthusiastically. "And the long life that the Vramen have always arrogated to themselves alone will belong to everyone."

"I am thinking," said Thol Orr slowly, "that it might be wise to study the effects of this radiation very carefully before using it on a wide scale—in fact, before we ourselves receive a definitive accumulation of it."

"What do you mean?" Wilson demanded. "Do you doubt that the radiation will have the effect they say?"

"I believe it will make us indefinitely longevous, just as they said," answered Thol Orr. "But radiation can have other effects too. I was struck by what Hammond said about there being no children here."

It took a moment for the implication to sink in. When it did there was a sudden gasp of horror from one of the women.

"Do you mean that the radiation could make us sterile?" exclaimed Lund.

"It could," Thol Orr said. "Radiation of those frequencies can have the most powerful effect on the genes."

"It's nonsense," said Wilson angrily.

"I wonder," muttered Quobba. "Nobody's ever heard of the Vramen having any children."

For a moment Hammond shockedly thought of the Tree of Life, and why the sons of men had been forbidden to eat of it. But then he thought of something else.

"No," he said to Thol Orr. "I don't believe it's so. Thayn spoke to Mar Kann of the children of the Third Men as though they actually existed."

"Furthermore," put in Wilson, "if sterility went with the secret of life the Vramen would certainly have told the whole galaxy so. That would have quieted down the Hooman demand for the secret."

The Algolian scientist nodded thoughtfully. "I hadn't thought of that. It does seem that sterility can't be it, though I feel sure there must be some powerful genetic effect from such radiation."

The talk went on, around and around in an endless circle

of hope, fear and worry until Hammond's head spun with it. He was tired of this gloomy world that they had risked so much to reach. He was tired of the endless speculation on what the Vramen would do and what the Third Men wanted. He was tired, period.

He went along the corridor to one of the austere little sleeping-chambers. It would not be dark for hours but he needed sleep. He stretched out on the plastic cot and slept heavily, until he dreamed that enormous six-fingered hands were reaching for him, grasping him. He awoke with a snort of repulsion and found that it was night, that the room was half dark, and that Iva Wilson was shaking him.

"What the devil—" he began, and then saw the white, strained look on her face. He sprang up. "What's the matter, Iva?"

"I wanted to talk to you," she said. "I'm worried, afraid, and I can't talk to father any more. He's been so obsessed for years with this secret of life that now he won't even listen to me."

Hammond drew her toward the open window. Out there in the night below them the city of the Third Men was illumined by a bluish, sourceless light that added a final touch of the oppressive to the black, massive buildings. From one big building far across the city came a blaze of white radiance that leaped and fell, and a distant, hammering clangor. It was a sound that Hammond had not heard here before and it rolled and echoed over the dark city lying quiet and still under the nebula sky.

Iva shivered. "I wish we had never come here. I do not like this place, and the eyes of these people horrify me."

"I agree," said Hammond. "They may look human, but they're not."

Iva turned to him, and in the half-light her soft face was pale and earnest.

"Will you tell me the truth about something, Kirk?"

"Of course. What?"

"Do you love Thayn Marden?"

155

Hammond felt exasperation. "For the Lord's sake, are you going to start that again?" he said impatiently. "I've explained over and over that that probe-record was a million miles off the truth—"

Iva nodded. "You have, but you have not convinced me, any more than Thayn herself can conceal from me that she loves you."

"Thayn in love with me?" he exclaimed. "Why, Iva, that's crazy. She hates me, despises me—"

"She loves you, I am certain of it," Iva said. "I watched her look at you, in the ship. And it must be a very great love indeed that can make her forget that she is a Vramen and you a Hooman."

Hammond felt overwhelmed, stunned. And out of his mental chaos rose the conviction, the certainty. He had fought it down all along. He had crowded it into his subconscious where only the encephaloprobe and Iva's keen eyes had been able to see it. He had deceived even himself by constant reiterations. But it was the truth. He had loved Thayn from their first meeting. He knew it now, and the knowledge of it would stay with him while he lived.

Iva seemed to read his catastrophic self-revelation in his face. She said, "I was sure that it was so. And since it is, there is something I must tell you."

"What?"

"This, Kirk. While you slept my father has made final, formal alliance with the Third Men. He turned over all the machines and metal we saved, and they were taken to that building."

And she nodded her dark head toward the distant building from which came the rising and falling radiance and the thunderous hammering.

Hammond felt startled, then angry. But before he could say anything, Iva added,

"The Third Men also wanted Thayn. They said it was vitally necessary to question her. My father turned her over to them hours ago."

156

Chapter 17

FOR A moment it seemed to Hammond that he could not breathe, that the words just spoken tied all his nerves into a freezing knot. All of his dread and dislike of the unhuman Third Men focused into an agonized fear for Thayn. Then a revulsion of rage came to him and he reached and grasped Iva's shoulders roughly.

"Wilson had no right to do that!" he said. "I was the one responsible for the capture of that ship and of Thayn—yet without a word to me, he lets them have her."

Iva hung her head. "He knew you would object so he would not let you be awakened." Then she added defensively, "But even though he's obsessed with the secret, he's not a cruel man. He made them promise they would not harm her either bodily or mentally."

"And a lot a promise would mean to those bastards," Hammond said savagely. He felt an anger and a hatred he had never felt before. The shattering realization of how he really felt for Thayn, followed so swiftly by awareness of her position of deadly peril, left him wild and shaken.

"Please, Kirk," whispered Iva. There were tears in her eyes and he became conscious of the furious strength with which he held her.

"I'm sorry, Iva," he said, releasing her. "It's not your fault. And you did come and tell me about it."

"My father and Gurth would call me a traitor for doing it," she said. "I don't love the Vramen. But I'm far more afraid of these strange Third Men. I can't help thinking that Thayn may have told the truth when she warned of terrible danger from these people."

Hammond tried to think. He had never felt more alone

157

and helpless yet he was utterly resolved to go to Thayn no matter who stood in the way.

"Do you know where she is?" he asked.

"Father said he turned her over to them in the same room where you talked this morning," Iva said. "I don't know where that is."

"I do," Hammond said. He made up his mind swiftly. He first made sure the shocker was still in his pocket. Then he asked, "The others are sleeping?"

Iva nodded. "I waited until they were so I could come and tell you."

"Then wait here, till I see whether I can get down to that room," he said. "If anyone awakes, don't tell them I've gone."

He went out into the corridor and passed the silent rooms in which the other Hoomen slept. He went around the corner of the next intersecting corridor, following the way they had come.

A Mech confronted him in the middle of the hallway. The square machine goggled at him with its staring lenses, and spoke in its toneless metallic voice.

"What are your wishes? If you desire to go anywhere, I am programmed to summon the masters."

Hammond stood, and the thing repeated the same words. When it started a third repetition, he turned and went back to the suite and room he had just left.

"We're practically prisoners," he told Iva. "They've got Mechs posted to watch us."

The anxiety in her pale face deepened. "Then these Third Men don't really trust us at all? I don't like it."

"I wish to Heaven we'd never come here," he muttered, "But I've got to get down there somehow."

He went to the window. The city Vonn slumbered with its strange blue illumination undimmed. Few were the sounds that came from its streets, but from far came the hammering of the radiant forge. Over it all arched the incredibly splendid glow of the nebula sky, dripping a soft radiance down upon this world at the heart of the mighty Trifid.

The great building in which they were seemed quiet. He could make out one or two shadowy figures moving in the paved court where the plastic fliers were kept, but that was all. He turned back to Iva and said quickly,

"I'm going down the wall. Help me fix a rope."

They tore strips from the cover on the pad of the cot. These were soon twisted together into a rude but serviceable rope. Hammond tied it to the cot-frame, tested its strength, and then dropped it out of the window and clambered over the sill. Iva leaned out and looked down at him, her face pale in the nebula glow, as he slid down the smooth black cement wall. He reached the ground and crouched for a moment at the base of the wall, holding the shocker ready in his hand and looking and listening. There was nothing, and after a moment he crept along the wall until he came to a door.

He opened it, peered in, then whipped inside quickly. He was in a softly lighted passage somewhere in the rear of the building. He tried to orient himself. If his somewhat hazy memories were right, the room in which they had held council with the Third Men that day was somewhere toward his right, in the part of the building near the court of the fliers.

Hammond started in that direction along the corridor. There was a cross-corridor a little way ahead, and he reconnoitered it carefully before running across it. Then as he started forward again, he heard voices from ahead, coming toward him.

Hammond poised, in an agony of indecision as to whether he should go boldly ahead and use the shocker or try to hide. One shout of alarm might be fatal and he chose the latter alternative. Running silently back to the cross-corridor he turned into it and hurried along it until he found a door that would open. He dodged into a dark, silent office. Crouched inside its doorway, he heard the murmur of the voices louder, and peered out and saw two of the tall Third Men across the corridor at the intersection. He heard their voices clearly for a moment.

"This is a bad night for the Vramen," one said, in high good humor.

"*And* the Fourth Men," said the other grimly.

They went on and their voices faded but Hammond remained for a moment, startled by the words. Who were the Fourth Men, he wondered? Was there still another race on Althar he hadn't heard about?

It was no time for speculation. He hurried to the intersection and went on again along the way from which the two had come.

"If I just don't meet any Mechs—," he thought, sweating.

He had an extreme apprehension of the wheeled robots, that could move so silently.

A feeling of despair came to Hammond as he worked on through the hallways of the sleeping building. He was not used to this sort of thing, he had never in his life tried to steal through a place in this furtive fashion. If only he could remember the way more clearly!

He heard a low, steady sound from ahead as he went on. He went more slowly, tensed up for anything. He saw a flicker of movement down the corridor he followed. A moment later, he felt ashamed of his own scariness. The movement was that of a moving ramp and the steady whirring sound came from it. With sudden hope, Hammond recognized this as the ramp up which the Mech had led them earlier in the day. If that was so, he knew the way now.

Yes. It was the way. In a minute he stood in front of the closed door of the room in which they had held council with the Third Men. His ear against the door, Hammond listened.

Nothing.

He touched the plate beside the door and it slid open.

The table and chairs were there, but no one now was there except at the end of the table Thayn Marden sat fettered in a chair. She was facing him, and her face was no longer dull and dazed, but it had a haggard, infinitely weary expression. Then her blue eyes opened wide as she saw Hammond come toward her.

"Behind you!" she cried.

He felt a breath of movement and spun around fast. One of the Mechs was rolling toward him from a corner of the room.

"No intruders are allowed here," said the hateful toneless voice. "I am programmed for lethal action after this warning. Withdraw."

Hammond levelled the shocker and pressed its stud. He had a wild hope that the electric charge might knock out the robot's circuits.

It didn't. Without repeating its warning, the Mech rolled swiftly toward him and its jointed crab-like arms flashed out to grasp him.

"On top of it, Kirk! Get on top of it!" cried Thayn.

Hammond had leaped to avoid the grasp of the powerful arms, but the Mech turned more swiftly than he and rolled toward him again.

Desperately, he slipped sidewise and then leaped up onto the flat square top of the Mech. Instantly the boxy robot began wheeling around the room with incredible swiftness, turning this way and that so suddenly that Hammond had to cling to avoid being thrown off. He thought at first it was consciously trying to throw him off, but then discovered that it was swiftly searching the room, over and over again. It was but a machine and when he was on top of it, it could not perceive him. Thayn's quick brain had glimpsed the one vulnerability of the thing.

Hammond, crouching on top of it, reached down with the shocker tube and smashed hard at one of the lenses in its front. The lens cracked and shivered. It was horribly like gouging out the eye of a living thing. He set his teeth and hammered at the other lens until it too broke. At once, as he had hoped, a safeguard relay came into play somewhere in the Mech and it stopped and was motionless.

Breathing hard, he went over to Thayn. Her wide blue

eyes looked up at him and her face seemed white and strange.

"Have they hurt you?" he asked.

She shook her head. "No, but I've been under hypnosis for hours while they questioned me." A flash of agony crossed her face. "They've never had a Vramen prisoner before and they've learned much from me—too much!"

He knelt down and examined the fetters that bound her wrists to the arms of the chair. They had no locks but consisted of spiral strips of very stiff plastic that wound around the wrist and chair-arm and held them tightly together. Hammond found them harder to uncoil than a stiff steel spring would have been.

Thayn said rapidly, "Kirk, I have to tell you this. If you free me I must try to get to my people in Sharanna and warn them what the Third Men plan."

He got one plastic spiral off, and started work on the other. He asked, without looking up,

"What do they plan?"

"Attack on Sharanna! They've tried it many times before but now, with the weapons they can forge out of the materials you Hoomen brought, they may succeed. Believe me, they're only using you; they regard you as animals."

"I believe that, all right," he muttered, struggling with the coiled plastic.

"They must not get out into the galaxy, Kirk! It's what we've always feared. And they'll do it, if they can smash us and—"

She stopped, but he remembered what he had overheard, and as he tugged hard at the second strip of plastic he asked, "Who are the Fourth Men, Thayn?"

She seemed startled by the question. "How could you— They're another race here on Althar. There's no time to explain now—those who questioned me only went to report, and they will return!"

He got the second strip of plastic off. But before Thayn could rise he grasped her wrists, and looked up into her face.

162

"You tricked me once, Thayn. Is this story of yours another trick?"

Her brilliant eyes looked down into his eyes. "No."

"You know why I came after you, don't you?"

She whispered, "Don't say it."

"Why not say it? I'm a fool. I'm fool enough to say I love you and to hope that you love me."

Her lips quivered. "I do, but—"

He waited for no more. He kissed her, and her lips answered his with an almost desperate passion. And then her head drew back.

"It is hopeless! We Vramen cannot really love anyone. I thought I had forgotten all such emotions."

"Why is it hopeless, Thayn?" he demanded passionately. "What's to keep us apart?"

"A gulf that is wider than space and deeper than time," she said, her eyes wet with tears. She tore away from him and rose to her feet.

Hammond's mind was a swirl of emotion. He knew the extreme and immediate danger in which they stood, and every word that Thayn had said reinforced his impression of unknown menace brooding on this world of endless life. And yet all he could think of was that he loved a woman who was not quite human with all his heart and that she returned his love.

Thayn's urgent voice recalled him. "We have only one chance of escape and that is to seize a flier. I can operate one—we've captured more than one of them in the past."

Hammond, trying hard to think clearly, hung back. "I can't leave my friends, Thayn."

"Will you help them by staying here to be killed by the Third Men? The only way you can help them now is by getting warning to Sharanna."

He still stood irresolute. "I betrayed them once for your sake."

She came and looked searchingly into his face. "Do you think I am lying to you now?"

He looked at her for an instant, and it was enough. In that moment something quiet and irrevocable happened inside his mind and heart. Nothing in the world would ever again be quite so important to him as was the woman who stood before him.

He said, "No. No more doubts. Let's go."

The supernal sky cast its soft light on them when they slipped silently out of the great building. They had met no one in the short corridor they had traversed, but Hammond thought that if those who had questioned Thayn returned soon, time was short. They paused, looking around, and then ran silently toward the wide paved court on which were parked the sleek plastic fliers.

No one moved among the machines. Hammond flung a glance backward, where the stark black mass of the building hung against the glowing sky, but saw no one behind them. They reached the nearest flier and Thayn was already climbing lithely into its cabin when a rasping and familiar metallic voice spoke from behind Hammond.

"Show authorization, please."

Hammond turned sharply and faced the box-like Mech and its glittering lenses. It spoke again.

"Show authorization, please. I am programmed to give alarm after this request."

From inside the cabin of the flier Thayn said rapidly,

"Stand clear of the wing."

Hammond and the Mech were just in front of the thick, stubby wing of the flier. He thought he knew what Thayn meant and he quickly stepped clear.

The Mech started to follow but at the same moment there was a whistling blast from the tail of the flier and it shot forward several feet. The wing hit the Mech and knocked it away. It rolled wildly out of control, banged into the next parked flier, and canted over on one side. But it was only damaged, not disabled. With mindless mechanical fidelity, it gave utterance to a shrieking alarm siren.

The flier had stopped after that brief leap forward. Hammond scrambled up into the cabin.

"Hang on!" said Thayn, from the control-seat.

Vertical jets whistled loudly underneath the belly of the craft, and it screeched upward into the night. As Hammond clambered unsteadily toward the seat beside Thayn, her hands moved and the flier went out of vertical into horizontal flight. Rocking and dipping, it rushed headlong across the black roofs of Vonn. Almost at once it was out from over the city and hurtling at rising speed over the plain. And then ahead of them the moss-forests showed as an endless stretch of dark clumps under the glowing sky.

"They'll follow," said Thayn. "Keep looking back."

Hammond did so, and after a while he described a swarm of shining specks in the sky far behind them. They rushed on and on, their flier attaining a speed that made its plastic walls hot with friction. They were flying over the moss-forests at such low altitude that their speed seemed dizzying. Yet as time passed the pursuing fliers drew ever closer.

"They know the operation of these craft better than I do and must have radar locked onto us by now," said Thayn.

Hammond looked at her, her clear profile tense but fearless in the hooded glow of the instrument-panel, her small hands quickly shifting the controls. He forgot imminent peril in a feeling of immense pride. She might not be an entirely human woman but she was more than any woman he had ever seen, and he had won her for his own.

She flashed him a quick glance. "We can't quite reach Sharanna, they'll get within range of us and use their weapons before we do. We've only one chance."

Hammond did not understand, and said so.

She was peering tensely ahead. "Black Lake should not be far ahead. If we can make them believe they've destroyed us—"

The softly lighted forest of great moss-clumps continued to unreel beneath them with appalling speed. Then a little way ahead a glint of gleaming water broke the weird forest.

"There it is!" said Thayn. "Open the cabin door and wait beside it till I get the autopilot on."

He did that, hanging to the edge of the open door with the wind screaming at him and trying to tear him loose. Then their speed decreased sharply and the flier sank lower, now only a few yards above the loftiest mosses.

"Take my hand and jump when I do!" Thayn said in his ear.

It seemed startlingly suicidal to Hammond but his pride and trust were so great that he made no objection. He gripped her small hand.

"Now!" she exclaimed, and threw herself out of the door with him.

Chapter 18

HAMMOND EXPECTED a violent shock when they hit the ground, but they did not hit it. Instead, he and Thayn plunged from the slow-moving flier into a big, soft, yielding mass only a few yards below. It was one of the great moss-clumps. Thayn had accurately estimated the exact moment of jumping so as to land in it.

As they rolled in the soft moss, the empty flier was winging on out over the dark waters of the lake. A moment later the pursuing fliers of the Third Men whistled by overhead. At their far greater speed they overtook the unoccupied machine out over the lake. There was no visible or audible evidence of weapons being used, but suddenly the empty flier was smashed into a wreck of broken plastic. It plummeted down and disappeared with a splash into the dark water.

"They will think we are still in it," Thayn murmured,

crouching down with Hammond in the moss. "Unless they suspect the trick."

For some time the fliers of the Third Men circled over the spot where the wreckage had sunk. Then, as though those in them were satisfied no one had survived the wreck, the fliers turned and raced whistling back in the direction of Vonn.

"We've escaped them," Thayn said with relief. Then, in the sky-glow, he saw her face fall. "But we're still a long way from Sharanna by foot, and we have no other way of travel."

He helped her climb down from the big clump. When they reached the ground, Thayn started without hesitation.

"We must skirt the lake and then strike straight north for the mountains," she said. "Sharanna is high in them."

It was weird, walking through the nighted moss-forests of Althar. The canopy of the nebula overhead cast its almost shadowless light down upon the silent, solemn mosses. Black Lake lapped and sucked gently along the shore they followed, and that was the only sound. There was no sign whatever of animal or bird life.

"Time is short, and we're many hours travel from Sharanna," said Thayn, quickening her stride.

"Even if the Third Men are preparing a weapon from the materials we brought, surely it'll take them some time," Hammond said.

She shook her head. "You don't comprehend their intellectual and scientific power. And while there are only a comparatively few Vramen in Sharanna to guard our base, the Third Men are many. They've waited long for a chance to strike at the Vramen—yes, and at their own children too."

Hammond felt puzzled. "You speak as though they were enemies of their children. Where are these children, anyway?"

Thayn looked at him, her face somber in the glow. "You were asking about the Fourth Men. I will tell you who they are. They are the children of the Third Men."

He stopped, astounded. "But why would they be called that? And why would they—" He took her hand, looking into her face. "I've had a feeling that there's some terrible mystery about this world. What is it, Thayn? Surely I have a right now to know."

"Yes," she said. "You have the right." Yet it seemed that for a moment she could not bring herself to speak. When she did, it was a question. "What did the Third Men tell you of their origin?"

He shrugged. "Not much. They said they were born on this world."

"So they were," she said. "Here they were born, many centuries ago. And their parents were the Vramen."

The enormity of the statement so stunned Hammond that it was moments before he could find his voice. And in those moments Thayn looked at him with the shadow of old tragedy strong on her white face.

"Those unhuman Third Men, the children of the Vramen!" he said finally. "Thayn, it's impossible."

"I wish it had been," she said. "But it is true. That is why they have their name. The Hoomen are the First Men, the first human species. We Vramen are the Second Men. The children of the Vramen, being a genetically different species, are the Third Men. And their children, genetically different from them in turn, are the Fourth Men."

She took his hand and urged him forward. "We must keep moving, Kirk. It is urgent that we reach Sharanna as soon as we can."

But as they walked, Thayn talked. And in Hammond's mind her words unfolded a tremendous and terrible saga.

"It began some two thousand years ago when some Hooman scientists, exploring the interior of the Trifid, came first to this star and its planet. They landed here on Althar, to study the strange radiation of the star. And after weeks of exposure, the unique radiation gave every cell in their bodies such an enhanced power of biological regeneration as to make them unaging, almost undying. They became the first Vramen."

"Jon Wilson told me that, back in the caverns," Hammond said. "And how they brought other picked Hoomen here to make them into Vramen too."

"Yes," said Thayn. "They had dreams of changing the whole Hooman race into Vramen, in time. They brought others here to Althar, they built Sharanna in the northern mountains as a base. And then—"

And then, Hammond learned, there had come a terrible revelation. A biological trap had been sprung. Children had begun to be born to the Vramen in Sharanna and they were not like either the Hoomen or the Vramen. They were a totally new human species, large in stature, with six-fingered hands, possessing brains and mental powers far beyond those of their parents. They were the Third Men. And the Vramen realized that though the rays of the star gave indefinite life, they also powerfully affected the genes, the units of heredity.

The Vramen, knowing the power of intense radiation to effect genetic changes, had been prepared for minor changes. They had very carefully ascertained that there would be no such changes of the genetic pattern as might cause monstrous births. But they had not been prepared for a great burst of evolutionary mutation in the human stock, one that created a new species from an old—as had happened many times in the past to other creatures.

Hammond gathered that the Vramen had at first hoped for great things from this godlike and big-brained new generation. But as the Third Men grew up, that hope had faded. For these were so completely a new species that they had not the same psychological make-up as their parents, at all. The emotions of their parents were quite alien to them. It was as though the too-sudden burst of evolutionary mutation had given them vast mental and physical development at the expense of what might be called spiritual development. For the Third Men, when they grew to maturity, were found to cherish the rooted conviction that they were destined to dominate everyone in the galaxy, Vramen and Hoomen alike, as inferior species of no great intelligence.

"So the Vramen came to a decision," Thayn said. "These children of theirs, this new and alien species, were a danger to all galactic peoples and must not be allowed ever to leave Althar. The Vramen acted before it was too late, against their sons and daughters—"

And, Hammond thought, what agonies of necessity and decision those few words must contain!

"—and forced them to leave Sharanna. The Third Men, totally devoid of filial emotion, set up a new city, Vonn. There their intellectual and scientific powers increased swiftly as the years passed. They would have come back then and tried to conquer their parents had their plans not been upset by a new turn of events."

The Third Men, it seemed, had intermarried and children had been born to them. The same deep power of the radiation that had caused the first mutation now caused another one. The children of the Third Men were not like their parents at all. They were still another new human species— the Fourth Men. And the Fourth Men had gone far down the road of change. They were closer to pure mind than any humans had ever been, overspecialized as to mind and with no capacity or inclination for any life of action. They cared nothing for the strife between their parents and grandparents. They desired only a life of quiet thought.

Their parents, the Third Men, had forseen that their children would be a new species and had deliberately planned to use its greater mental powers for their own purposes. But the Fourth Men, hating action and ambition, would not let themselves be so used. When they matured they deserted their parents and went off to found a strange new city, and refused to have contact with either Vramen or Third Men.

"And there," Thayn said, "they have lived ever since, engaged in the pure mental research that is their purpose in life."

Hammond felt overwhelmed by this epic history of mutation running wild with the human stock on this world of unending life.

"And did the Fourth Men produce still another mutation?" he asked.

Thayn shook her head. "No. The Fourth Men are sterile. They are the end-products of human evolution on this world. But since, like us Vramen and the Third Men, they have indefinite life, they have lived on ever since."

Many things became clear to Hammond, as though illumined by a terrible lightning-flash. He knew now why Mar Kann had mockingly said of Thayn, *"I had hoped that she might be someone very dear to me,"* and why Thayn had bitterly answered, *"I was spared that shame."* He knew now why her reference to the "beloved children of the Third Men" had so stung Mar Kann.

Thayn added somberly, "And that is the reason why we Vramen have kept the Hooman races away from Althar and the secret of life."

"But, good God, why didn't you just tell the whole galaxy the truth?" exclaimed Hammond. "People wouldn't want any part of the secret of long life if they knew what went with it."

Thayn looked at him. "Wouldn't they?"

And when Hammond thought about it, he became less sure. The will to live was the deepest, strongest human trait. Suppose you are an ordinary man or woman, and you learn that there is a way by which you can live indefinitely. You are told that there is a catch in it, that your children will be different, bigger and brainier than you are. Would that stop you from grabbing at long life? He had to admit to himself that it would not. And when you had children who were of the new species, the Third Men, they too would want to live indefinitely and would hunger for the rays of the star of life, and so would come the next mutation and you ended up with the Fourth Men, a sterile race that would be the blind-alley end of humanity.

"You're right, Thayn," he said. "They'd come flocking to this star like moths to a flame."

"And the flame would consume the races of men, in time," she said. "It would take very long but finally there would be only the Fourth Men, and after them, nothing."

After a moment she added, "There is one thing sure and that is that the Third Men are a danger not only to the Vramen but to the Fourth Men. And out of that danger we may draw salvation yet."

Thayn fell silent as they tramped on through the moss-forests under the softly glowing sky. And Hammond's mind was so feverishly considering what he had heard, that he did not even notice her silence. He thought again of the Tree of Life that had been forbidden to men. It seemed to him that it was not by chance alone that this unique Star of Life had come to being inside the depths of the great nebula where it was difficult to attain. But men had attained it and to their sorrow. And now he, Kirk Hammond, had attained it also and that brought up a question in his mind.

Hours passed before Thayn stopped and broke her silence. "We had better rest. We still have a long way to go."

Hammond thought that very probably she was less tired than he. He sat down with her by a great moss-clump and looked at her clear profile. Then she turned suddenly and said,

"Do you feel differently toward me now that you know what a different species I belong to?"

He stared. "Is that what you've been brooding about? Once and for all, Thayn—no!"

He took her by the shoulders but she drew back from him, and shook her head. Her face was tragic.

"It is no good, Kirk. You are a Hooman and will want a wife and children in the normal Hooman way. And no Vramen can marry in that sense or have children. We renounce all that when we accept the rays of the Star."

"But Thayn—", he began, but she rushed on.

"I made that renunciation two hundred years ago, and I knew what it entailed. The Vramen who invited me to become one of their caste told me that terrible history of what happened two thousand years ago, just as I have told it to you. I understood the conditions, and I came with them to Althar and became a Vramen."

He put his hand over her lips. "Let me speak. You're forgetting something. You're forgetting that I'll become a Vramen too, when I've lived under the Star long enough."

"No," she whispered. "You must not. You would regret the decision in time and would come to hate me."

He did not answer that in words. He took her into his arms and held her. Dark and solemn above them towered the ungainly moss and all about them was the silence of the weird forest and the soft radiance of the unearthly sky. A strange place, and a strange fate that had brought these two together from across space and time to cling blindly to each other.

"Thayn, Thayn—"

Chapter 19

SHARANNA OF the Vramen rose before them late in the afternoon, when the Star of Life was low in the western sky and its light was muted and darkened, striking the high peaks and the single great soaring pylon with shafts of sombre purple and angry red and an ugly green like spilled poison. Hammond shivered. It seemed an ill omen to have his first look at the Vramen city in this light, as though it were a place already under the shadow of destruction.

Whether Thayn felt that way or not he could not tell. Her face was set and pale, a mask that had not changed expression during all that long and bitter day. She was as remote from him as though she were on another star, and her remoteness hurt him, and yet he sensed that her withdrawal was rather because she did love him than that she did not. Bewildered and unhappy, he had tried many times to break through that barrier, but finally he had had to give up and walk beside her as silent as she was.

Now the tall pylon of Sharanna was in front of him, and the air was heavy with clotted color and the mountains veiled themselves in bloody mists, cold watchers around an arena where the victim waited for—what was the old phrase?—the moment of truth.

Thayn walked faster, faster, leaving him behind. Hammond forced himself to keep up.

There was a spaceport with perhaps half a dozen ships parked on it and a series of buildings with a slim radar tower rising above them. The pylon was beyond the port in a splendid upland valley, its disciplined lines contrasting strongly with the rough wild rock of the surrounding peaks. There were no defenses that Hammond could see, but Thayn spoke to him suddenly for the first time in hours and put out her hand.

"Stay close by me. Now—step where I do—exactly, Kirk!"

She held his hand and he walked with her in a curious sort of ritual pattern, so many steps to this point, so many more to that, and he knew that she was leading him on the equivalent of a marked path through a mine-field. Probably it was only his nervous imagination that made him sense a quivering of energy in the air around him. Thayn's hand was cold in his, and he was ashamed because his own palm became slippery with sweat.

She released him at last. They were close to the pylon now. Hammond wiped his hands furtively on his jacket, and saw the Vramen men coming toward them, running.

Things happened quickly after that. Hammond had no part of them because this was Thayn's world and these were her people, but he felt the impact of them none the less.

174

He found himself swept into the pylon almost before he knew it, while voices rose and echoed around him, hard and sharp in the quiet corridors, and then he was alone in an antechamber with two Vramen men who watched him but did not speak. He sat, and felt the whole mighty pylon-city stir and wake around him, clangorous with bells and footsteps. The ugly light of the setting sun mocked him through the window.

In the next room, beyond a white door, Thayn was talking to the leaders of the Vramen.

He did not know how long it was before the door opened again. Probably not long, because time had run out on the men of Sharanna, who had always had so much of it before. Thayn stood there and beckoned him to come in.

Five men sat around a table. They seemed older than any of the Vramen Hammond had seen before—not in any sense aged, but more mature, as though the passing of many centuries had worn the lines deeper in their faces. Their eyes were very wise, frighteningly so, but there was more than wisdom in them now. They looked at Hammond as men might look at a headstrong child who has set their house on fire with forbidden matches.

"It is very hard," one of them said to him, "not to want to kill you." He rose suddenly and turned his back on Hammond as though he needed to fight for self-control.

"I had to tell them how it all happened," Thayn said.

Hammond said nothing. There did not seem to be any words to cover the enormity of his mistake, and yet he felt that it had been an honest mistake and in some part due to the Vramen themselves.

Apparently the man behind the desk had had some such thought himself, for he turned around again and said harshly,

"I suppose this was bound to happen sometime. Probably it's a miracle it hasn't happened sooner." He looked hard at Hammond. "Thayn tells us we have you to thank for getting her away from the Third Men—otherwise we would have had no warning at all. Now there's another choice for you to make. Go ahead, Thayn."

Her voice sounded very tired when she spoke, and she would not look at him.

"I'll tell you this first of all, Kirk, so that there won't be any mistake. Your life may depend on what you decide to do. We're getting our ships off the ground at once, to keep them out of the hands of the Third Men. You can go with them. Or you can stay here and take your chances—"

"What will you do?" he asked, interrupting her.

"Stay. But you—"

"I'll stay too," he said.

She shook her head impatiently. "Hear me out, Kirk. We have decided to ask the Fourth Men for help. That sounds easy, but it isn't. The Fourth Men do not allow trespassers. Anyone, Third Man or Vramen, who crosses their boundary is subjected to a withering mental assault that stuns him and drives him out before he even gets close to the city, let alone has a chance to speak. I thought—"

She hesitated, and the Vramen at the table looked at her and she sighed and went on.

"I thought that you might be our one hope of gaining entrance to their city. If you were willing to try."

"I don't quite see—" said Hammond.

"Your background, Kirk. Your origin. The Fourth Men are interested in every field of knowledge. They might be interested enough in you—in what they would see in your mind—to let you come in."

One of the Vramen at the table said, "I don't think we Vramen, or you Hoomen either, can survive as free individuals without their help. The Third Men have the capacity now to overrun us all. Keeping our ships out of their hands is only a delaying action. Your friends have provided them with metals and atomic power. They will start element-building processes, and it won't be long before they have ships of their own. They'll be free of the galaxy, and there's no power that can stand against them.

"Except the Fourth Men," Hammond said.

"Except the Fourth Men. If they will. If we can persuade them to, now, before the situation gets beyond them. They don't care what happens to us or to the galaxy. They may just possibly be made to care what happens to them."

Through the high window Hammond could see the spaceport lights flare on, white in the curdled dusk. He felt an enormous weariness, a homesickness that was like an actual physical pain. He had shot everything he had in the fight to get out here and take away the secret of life from the Vramen. Victory had turned into a cruel nightmare and it was all for nothing, and he was where he had never had any business to be. He was tired. He wanted to go home, to hide himself under the little sky of Earth and forget that there was anything beyond it.

He turned suddenly and caught Thayn looking at him, and she flushed and dropped her gaze. He smiled, because he knew that she had been hoping against all reason that he would say No and go out with the ships where he would be safe for at least a while, perhaps for the rest of this life, since even the Third Men would require some time to conquer a galaxy.

He said to the Vramen leader, "I don't really have much choice, do I? Does somebody go with me, or do I try it alone?"

"I go with you," Thayn said, and stood beside him.

The Vramen leader said, "No. The Fourth Men might let two into their city, but certainly not more, and the second one must obviously be myself. They wouldn't treat with anyone else."

Thayn said furiously, "But Rymer, I thought—"

Rymer shook his head. "You know how they detest emotion. I'm afraid they would find you and the Hooman in combination far too upsetting."

This was so obviously a rebuke that Hammond bristled up and started to say something. But Thayn put a hand on his arm and said quietly, "Good luck, Kirk." She smiled and went out through the white door, walking erect with her head high. Hammond called after her but she did not turn nor pause, walking away from him across the room that was filled with the last blood-purple and blackish green of the sunset, hideous light like the light of an evil dream. Her white flesh and her pale hair glimmered, became indistinct. It was as though she were vanishing like the stereo-image on the ship, and a sudden fear caught at Hammond. He shouted her name and then he started to run after her, but Rymer was in front of him barring his way, and Rymer said,

"We have very little time."

In less than a quarter of an hour their flier was hurtling eastward under the glow of the nebular sky. The dark mountains dropped behind them. For quite a while Hammond could see the lights of the pylon, and the pillars of flame where the ships took off one by one for the safety of space. Then even those were gone.

Rymer said, not unkindly, "You may as well sleep while you can."

Hammond did not think he would ever sleep again. He kept seeing Thayn moving away from him, vanishing in the ominous light, and there was a coldness around his heart that would not go away. And somewhere over the dark land the blue lights burned and the forges clanged in the city of Vonn, hammering out the sword that would destroy Sharanna. He wondered if the Hoomen there understood yet what they had done. He wondered if they were still alive to understand anything.

He wondered if any of them would be alive this time tomorrow.

Rymer shook him and he knew that he had slept, in spite of himself. The flier had landed on a barren plain, where there was not a rock or a tree to break the emptiness except where one great bulk rose up ahead, a flat-topped mesa dim in the night-shine of the nebular sky.

"We'll have to go the rest of the way on foot," Rymer said. And added, "As far as we go."

Hammond supposed that Rymer was afraid of crashing the flier when the mental attack of the Fourth Men came. He followed the Vramen out onto the plain and looked around, puzzled.

"I don't see any city."

Rymer pointed to the dark bastion of the mesa. "There. Inside the rock. A thousand tunnels, a million holes. They live like ants in a hill that can't be broken, stepped on, or burned." He shook his head, looking like any man preparing to do a necessary but hateful act. "Come on," he said. "Forget Thayn if you can. Think about your past, the world and the people you knew ten thousand years ago. Think hard."

They started toward the mesa.

Hammond thought about Earth, the old Earth that was lost to him forever, the sounds and the colors, faces, voices, streets, the rockets, the launching pad, life and death fading out together in the cold moon. And underneath these thoughts he knew where he was and what he was doing, and he tasted fear in his mouth like liquid copper.

He was not at all prepared for what happened. It was a cloudburst, a hurricane, earthquake, the slapdown of a million G's in a crazy rocket going right out of the universe, and all of it soundless, all of it in his head. He couldn't stand it. He couldn't fight it. He couldn't do anything but turn blindly, screaming, and run run run—

He had fallen and there was dirt in his mouth.

The flier sat all by itself on the plain far ahead of him. A dark twisted shape crouched some ten feet away to his left and he saw that it was Rymer, folded over his own knees. The stunning agony was gone from Hammond's brain but there was still something wrong, something strange in his head. He could feel a presence there, turning over his memories like the pages of a book. He made an instinctive effort to get up and run again and found that he was unable to move. Tremors of fear and revulsion shook him. He was very cold.

Somebody said, "You are permitted to enter the city."

Hammond got up. The presence had withdrawn from his mind, leaving only a thin thread of itself behind. The thread pulled him gently but firmly toward the mesa. He walked. Rymer walked beside him. Hammond could hear his heavy breathing. Neither one of them spoke. Hammond's thoughts were strangely confused. He was not sure of anything.

The wall of the mesa rose above them, black and impenetrable. There was no sign of an opening anywhere, but Hammond and Rymer walked without hesitation to a certain place. A small portion of the rock opened quietly on pivots.

They entered the city of the Fourth Men.

Some of Hammond's daze left him. He blinked in the soft light and looked around. He and Rymer were in a very small room with opaque glassy walls. It pressed hard against their feet and he knew it was a lift taking them up to higher levels. He imagined that with the lift drawn up there would be no way for an invader to get beyond that single doorway even if he could find it.

An impregnable ant-hill, Rymer had said. But things had changed. They were forging a hammer in Vonn that would smash this rock to shards.

The lift stopped. A section of the wall slid back and they stepped out into a corridor that had the same gleaming glassy walls and the same glow of indirect light, so that it seemed to plunge ahead of them in an endless shining tube. It was far too small for his size. He bent his head and shuffled forward along the shining floor. Rymer came after him, his knuckles almost brushing his feet.

Someone stood in the corridor ahead of them.

At first Hammond thought it was a child. It was perhaps four feet tall, dressed in a single brief garment. The body had the slim unformed beauty of childhood, before sex has begun to make any significant changes. The head was large in proportion to the body, not much more than is normal in a child. The features were a little cold in expression but very handsome. Only the eyes were completely alien, huge and deep and of a strange pale color as though they were accustomed to looking at things forever hidden from the eyes of man.

"Reverend grandfather," the small person said to Rymer, with icy irony. "I am Clede." The creature looked at Hammond with considerable interest. "This is the first Hooman I have seen. Its brain is rudimentary but does contain information of a unique sort. It will take us only a few moments to extract and record. In the meantime, reverend grandfather—"

"In the meantime," said Rymer harshly, "you had better look inside my mind and see why this Hooman was brought here."

"Oh," said Clede, "that has already been done. I was about to say that three of our number will listen to you while the Hooman is being examined. Please walk softly. Noise is very distracting to thought."

Clede led the way along the corridor and into other corridors, moving like thistledown. Hammond, feeling gross and clumsy, followed after with Rymer. On either side of the corridors now he saw that there were cells in the rock at regular intervals, lined with the glassy glowing substance and closed by transparent panels. In each one of these child-sized cells a small figure sat in an attitude of profound thought.

"Since we have complete telepathic communication," Clede murmured, "we are able to link a number of our units together for group effort on larger problems. Most of us are so occupied. Only the few of us engaged in private research are free to deal with you, and even so it is a painful interruption. We will make it as brief as possible."

Rymer started to say something forceful and then shut his jaws again with an audible snap. In spite of himself Hammond was amused. This chief of the Vramen, so vastly superior to himself, was humble and unsure in the presence of this little pattering creature. Then he wondered what he was amused about. It was not funny at all. It was terrifying to realize that his life and Thayn's and the lives of countless people both Vramen and Hooman, now and in the future, depended on the whim of these cool unhuman minds. He looked at the childlike forms that sat with folded hands and unseeing eyes in their monastic cells, and he had a sudden conviction that they could not be moved, that they would sit there until the world fell literally crashing on their heads, too far withdrawn from the realities of life to know or care until it was too late.

"In here, reverend grandfather," said Clede, pointing to an open panel in the wall. Hammond saw a chamber beyond in which three of the Fourth Men sat waiting. Rymer looked at Hammond, took a deep breath, and went in. The panel closed.

"Come," said Clede. The small mouth curved with the distant shadow of a smile. "There's nothing to fear. You will not be harmed in any way. Your thoughts are quite clear to me. You wonder whether I am male or female. You wonder how it is possible to live without sex, without love, without emotion. Open your mind to me and listen and perhaps I can make you understand a little, a very little, for your mind is unformed, so limited—"

The little figure drew away from him along the shining corridor and Hammond followed it. It danced like a will-o'-the-wisp in a glowing mist and now Hammond floated lightly after it, calm and unafraid. All fear, all feeling had left him, and he was only aware in the most detached fashion when he came into a quite large circular place where there were rows and rows of cells rising in tiers, each one with a figure in it dimly seen.

"This is our group memory," Clede whispered. "Stand here."

Hammond stood, and the living memory bank of the Fourth Men emptied his brain of knowledge like a cup. There was no pain. He was not aware when it was over. He was not aware of anything at all until he found himself walking down the corridor again and there was somebody with him. Not Clede. Oh, yes. Rymer.

They got into the lift again and went down and out the door of pivoted stone, which closed behind them and was not. They walked toward the flier and did not speak. Hammond's mind was totally incurious, at peace.

It was not until they were almost back to the flier that that muffling influence suddenly vanished. It was as though the Fourth Men had kept them in that state so as not to be disturbed by the noise of their emotions. The two men looked at each other like sleepers suddenly wakened, and then Hammond cried,

"What did they say? Will they help?"

Rymer's voice was edged and bitter with helpless rage. "They said they would look into it. They do not like to be disturbed. It annoys them excessively. But because there is a possibility that the Third Men may now constitute a threat to their continued peace, they will look into it."

"When?" said Hammond desperately. "What will they do?"

"Nothing," said Rymer, "unless they feel that the threat to them is actual. They do not like to be disturbed." He looked at the mesa. "I hope they are disturbed. I hope they—No. I'm getting worse than a Hooman. I didn't know I had so much childish emotion left after two thousand years."

He turned and ran for the flier.

As they took off Hammond repeated, "Two thousand years?"

"Yes," said Rymer. "I was one of the first. My blood runs in the Third Men, and through them in the Fourth. I was in at the beginning."

The flier hurtled westward and behind them the Star of Life rose up and it was day.

This time, on the way back, Hammond did not sleep. He sat hunched forward in the seat of the flier, straining his eyes for the first glimpse of Sharanna.

The way seemed very long. The Star of Life climbed in

many-colored splendor up the sky and the empty miles reeled back under the flier. And all the time Hammond's heart pounded heavy and slow and there was a cold sickness in him.

They came to Sharanna shortly before noon, and it was already too late.

Chapter 20

IN THE sky low above the mountains there poised and whirled and slashed a colossal scimitar of light. The hand of a god might have wielded that stupendous sword of radiance but there was no hand visible. There was only the great blade of destruction that slashed through peaks and sent them tumbling in avalanches of broken rock, that turned and came back and sliced again, cutting through all in its path. Even in that first horrifying glimpse, Hammond knew that its radiance must be a force somehow potent to dissolve the subtle bonds between electrons and sub-electrons and thus shatter the lattice-work of particles and emptiness that matter really is.

Up from the hidden defences all around Sharanna struck the weapons of the Vramen, the savage, raving sheets and bolts of force, the leaping missiles that exploded in hellish flowers of flame. But the sword in the sky disdained them. Some remote-controlled flying device at its heart might generate it but that was beyond the reach of Vramen weapons, shielded by the destructiveness it created. No empty boast had been the promise of the Third Men that they could build a thing of terror when they had the materials! Out of long-cherished plans of a superhuman science they constructed and sent this sword that was hacking Sharanna to bits.

Riven in twain was the great pylon that had been a city in itself, and it stood like a broken tombstone in its own wreckage. And down upon it again came the inexorable blade of radiance, cutting through the shattered building to quarter it, sweeping on in destruction.

"Make it stop, oh God, make it stop!" cried Hammond. "Thayn—"

But it would not stop, it danced in the sky and exultantly flashed down again and again until all the mountains were a broken wilderness of stone around the broken stronghold of the Vramen. Then the sword of light faded swiftly from the sky.

"Rymer," said Hammond. "*Rymer!*"

Rymer was sitting with his hand loose upon the controls of the flier and his face was a stony mask. He had seen the destruction of Sharanna, the end of his personal world and era, and he could not hear Hammond at all.

Hammond yelled in his ear, then cursed and beat him with his fists and pointed away to the southward where a covey of black midges had appeared.

"Land!" Hammond yelled. "Damn you, land—they stayed back in safety till now but now they're coming!"

Rymer turned a perfectly blank look upon him. Then he moved his hands on the controls. He sent the flier down toward the broken stone wreckage of Sharanna. He handled the craft with the stiff mechanical perfection of a robot pilot, and he brought them down smoothly onto the rock in front of the shattered pylon.

Hammond leaped out. Already the midges had become big and black in the sky and they were beginning to circle and drop, whistling like hawks. Hammond left Rymer standing beside the flier white-lipped, and ran.

The air had a scorched smell. The ground was partly fused. He passed a queer splotch and realized that it was a puddle of melted steel. Wreckage lay everywhere, broken fragments of stone and metal.

There were bodies, too.

None of them were Thayn. None, at least, that were still recognizable. He ran on, heading for the pylon. He did not know why. She might have been anywhere on the plain, anywhere under the terrible blade of that apocalyptic sword. He sobbed as he ran. Behind him the black fliers fell whistling out of the sky.

He went into the shattered pylon.

The doorway was broken, but inside there was a hundred feet of the high corridor that was undamaged. Amid the universal destruction it gave a curious illusion of peace and wholeness.

He saw Thayn.

She sat quite alone in that long and empty place, her back resting against the mass of shattered, fallen stone and metal at its end. It was as though she had sat here waiting for him, and when she saw him she smiled and said his name. She looked somehow like a broken doll and then he saw that her whole side had been crushed in and that she kept it pressed against the broken stone.

"Kirk," she said, and he went down on his knees beside her and took her in his arms.

"You must have help," he said. "I'll get help somewhere." Though where he would find it in fallen Sharanna he did not know, and anyway it was no use, no use at all, and he knew it. Only the unhuman vitality of the Vramen had kept her alive this long.

She held him close, close against her and the perfume of her hair mingled with the smell of burning.

"There's no help," she said. "Even the Vramen die sometime. I've lived a long time, but none of it was really good until the end, until I met you and loved like any Hooman woman—"

He could not say anything but her name, holding her as though he would keep the life in her with his hands, and all the time it was running out of her with every breath.

"I wish I could know that you'll be safe," she whispered.

"I'll be all right."

She said suddenly, "Kirk!"

Her face had changed, it was no longer the proud face of Thayn of the Vramen, it had a scared, shy, little-girl look and she clung hard to him. And then her hands fell away, and he held her tightly and knew that he was holding nothing at all.

He sat there, not moving. He heard the whistling of many fliers landing and he knew that Sharanna had indeed fallen, but Thayn was dead and beside that the fall of empires was nothing. He wished that he was dead too. He wished that he had stayed forever on his icy throne, staring blindly at the stars and never waking again at all. He sat there in the shattered pylon, until there came a sound so strange that it roused him from his stupor.

The sound of laughter.

Hammond got slowly to his feet and walked down the hall and into the brilliance of the opal sun. He heard a man's voice shouting, and then there was much more laughter.

Out in a clear space amid the wreckage of Sharanna, Rymer stood and raised his voice in curses at the Third Men. He was a grotesque, gesticulating figure, all the dignity of his long living fallen away from him, as he raved and raged.

And the Third Men laughed. There were very many of them in wrecked Sharanna now, some of them alertly searching the debris, full of the business of conquest, others rounding up the few stunned Vramen who alone survived. But a group of them stood here in the open facing Rymer. They were tall and godlike, full of power, full of confidence. They had triumphed, and the highest note of their triumph was the screaming, raging man before them, and they were happy. They laughed.

They had killed Thayn.

Hammond, slowly and with heavy purpose, began to move out toward them. He might kill one, only one—but that would be something.

Rymer stopped screaming and looked blankly toward

Hammond. The Third Men looked too, and Hammond saw their faces become hard and ruthless.

Then he realized that they were not looking at him at all. He turned.

From behind him, from beyond the shattered pylon, four childlike figures were coming. They were Fourth Men, and he thought that one of them was Clede.

There was a silence, and the Third Men gathered and Clede and his three small companions went toward them. How the four had come to Sharanna Hammond could not guess. They might have landed in a flier behind the broken plyon. Or they might well, he thought, know the ways of teleportation.

The four little figures faced the godlike crowd of their parents, and Rymer stared and was silent and Hammond watched from where he had stopped. So at last all of the four human species had come together on this world, and overhead the Star of Life blazed with its peacock fires in the sky and cared nothing for the tragedy it had made.

Clede's voice was soft and bitter as he spoke to the Third Men. "You are happy. You have filled Althar with war and confusion, and you think it good."

Holl Gorman spoke from among the Third Men. "Our children are come to lesson us—listen carefully, all!" He laughed scornfully and then his eyes blazed. "Dreamers, fools besotted with too much thought, it is you who shall learn now! We fathered you. Your brains were to be for our use, and now they shall be. You will serve us from now on in proper filial piety, or perish. Go back and tell your weakling people that!"

"There is no need," murmured Clede. "The minds of all are linked with ours at this moment. And we are all agreed. You are our fathers but you must not destroy us and yourselves, and all peace and thought on Althar. We must save you from that—now!"

A shade of anxiety flashed into Holl Gorman's face and

188

he opened his mouth to shout, but before he could utter a sound it happened.

Hammond felt in his mind the explosion of a mental force that seemed to rive his brain. Yet even as he staggered and cried out, he felt that it was only the fringes of that explosion that reached him, that it was directed elsewhere. He shut his eyes and pressed his hands against them. He knew—and this was a knowledge not born of his own mind— that it was the immeasurable massed mental power of all the distant Fourth Men, channelled through Clede and his three companions, whose edge he felt.

As swiftly as it had come that violent mental explosion faded. Hammond opened his eyes and blinked dazedly.

For nothing had happened.

Nothing? It seemed to him that there was something odd now about the Third Men.

They no longer stood defiant and lordly. Some of them smiled vacantly. Some of them sat down in the dust and played with little bits of charred destruction. Some wept, or stumbled about whimpering like very small, lost babies.

"My God," said Rymer. "You—"

Clede turned on him and Rymer stopped as though he had been struck in the face.

"What we have done is not for your sake!" said Clede in a bitter voice. "Remember that, reverend grandparents—not for you!"

There was a cold and terrible anger in Clede's face and it was reflected in the eyes of his companions, pale and strange. They looked at the stumbling, creeping, infantile creatures who had been the Third Men. Hammond looked at them, and felt sick.

"We have not blasted our fathers' minds," said Clede. "We have only wiped them clean—of hate and hunger, of all hope and all memory. They are infants again—mentally they are as when you birthed them, but they are our charges now, and we will care for them and teach them and perhaps make better men out of them than you did. But it was done for them and for us—not for your Vramen whose ambition for immortality brought us all to this!"

Clede added, "You have done enough harm here on Althar. We will have no Vramen or Hoomen here. Recall the ships you sent forth, and leave in them. And come here no more."

"But—" said Rymer.

Clede put out a small hand and touched the cheek of a Third Man who played babylike in the dust beside him. It was a gesture curiously compounded of tenderness and cruel mockery. He did not repeat his words, but he looked at Rymer steadily.

Rymer took a step backward. "Very well," he said. "We'll go."

Clede smiled. He looked up at the Star of Life, the peacock blaze of it beating on his face, catching in uncanny flashes in his eyes.

"It's an evil star," he murmured. "Men have found it twice now, they will find it again. They'll hunt for it, or the legend of it, as long as its rays hold life. Well, I think we can end all that. It should not be too hard for us to alter its gravitational field so that it draws the nebula dust in upon itself, to smother it in burning dust so its rays no longer have that power. Then we shall have peace here."

He turned his back on the Vramen and stretched out his hands to the Third Man who sat beside him in the dust.

"Come," he said gently. "It is time to go home."

After that, time stopped for Hammond. He sat in the shadow of the broken pylon and looked at nothing and there was a great weariness in him. Ships landed, and Vramen came and spoke to him, and he would not answer. Time passed and others came and spoke to him, in the voices of Iva and Quobba and Thol Orr, voices shaken and wild telling how the Fourth Men had come to Vonn and how the Third Men there had been made like children and the Hoomen had been sent to Sharanna. Hammond heard their voices and they were like voices in a dream, and he saw through a gray mist.

The mist lifted, finally. He was in a Vramen ship that droned through space, and when he looked through the scanner he could see quite clearly. He saw the Star.

It blazed in triumphant opal glory, pouring its iridescence upon its little planet. He did not think it would blaze long. He thought that if men ever came again they would find it drowned in dust as Clede had promised, and so the long fight between Vramen and Hooman was over. Men would no longer search for Althar and Thayn would have the quiet of eternity around her.

"Hammond—"

Quobba spoke beside him. He could see the others, Iva looking earnestly toward him, Jon Wilson sitting sunken and sad amid the wreck of his long hopes. But of them only Quobba had quite dared approach him.

"It's not the end of everything," he said. "They'll take us back to Kuum, but the way things turned out I think they'll soon let us go. You'll forget—"

"No," said Hammond.

Quobba shuffled. "Well, maybe not. But remember, there's all space to roam, and it'll be free now that the Vramen have nothing more to hide. And you're a spaceman, one of the first of us all. That's something to hang to, Hammond."

"Is it?" asked Hammond. "Was it such a good thing to conquer space? We thought it would be, back in the Twentieth Century. But was it?"

He looked out into the blind light and darkness of the universe but there was no answer there for his question. There would never be an answer, for it was not a matter of good or ill. Man could not choose now, he had made his choice long ago when as half-man he had looked up at the stars and coveted them. He would look farther yet with desire, upon galaxies and realms beyond present thinking, and would struggle for them, falling into many a cosmic trap like the one here, and always striving pitifully to snatch individual happiness before he died in that struggle.

It came to Hammond that he had had the happiness which so many grasped for and missed. He had had to come far across time and space to find it and he had had it only for an hour, a day, but he had had it, and he had the memory of it, and of a sudden he was strangely content.